HAPPINESS IS EASY

Edney Silvestre

Translated from the Brazilian Portuguese by Nick Caistor

BLACK SWAN

TRANSWORLD PUBLISHERS
61–63 Uxbridge Road, London W5 5SA
www.transworldbooks.co.uk

Transworld is part of the Penguin Random House group of companies
whose addresses can be found at global.penguinrandomhouse.com

First published in Great Britain in 2014 by Doubleday
an imprint of Transworld Publishers
Black Swan edition pubished 2015

A felicidade é fácil first published in Brazil by Record, 2011

The translator of this work received a grant from the Programme of Residency of Foreign
Translators in Brazil, from the Ministry of Culture of Brazil/National Library Foundation.

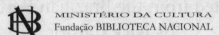

MINISTÉRIO DA CULTURA
Fundação BIBLIOTECA NACIONAL

A CIP catalogue record for this book
is available from the British Library.

ISBN
9780552778862

Typeset in 11.75/15 pt Minion by Falcon Oast Graphic Art Ltd.
Printed and bound by CPI Group (UK) Ltd, Croydon, CR0 4YY.

In memory of Edmond Silvestre

Lorsque l'enfant était enfant,
Il ne savait pas qu'il était enfant,
Tout pour lui avait une âme
Et toutes les âmes étaient une.

Peter Handke/Wim Wenders,
Wings of Desire

1

THE BOY WAS startled when the limousine pulled up along-side him, and the man at the wheel waved for him to get in. The boy smiled, because it was in his nature to smile and show gratitude for a kindness done or promised. The boy smiled in anticipation of his pleasure at climbing into that shiny dark-blue car, with its soft tan-leather seats.

The boy smiled because he had learned that by smiling and tilting his head to the left a little, as he was doing now, and looking at adults with the blue eyes he had inherited from his Pomeranian great-grandparents, he almost always received a smile in return. A smile from his parents' bosses, a pat on his fine blond hair, sometimes a few coins or even a banknote slipped into the palm of his hand by the man with dark-brown skin, the owner of that vast house with such high walls where his parents worked. He smiled because that was what he believed made the men in black who were constantly patrolling the house hurry up, as they were the only ones able to open the gate he left by every morning to go to school in this big city where his mother and father had finally brought him.

He smiled because that was what he had done in the months while he waited for them to come and get him as they had promised. Thanks to his smile, he was rewarded with a little more food or a little less punishment when he did something wrong, like the afternoon he opened the sheep-pen and ran up into the hills with the sheep. He didn't shout or make any noise as other children would have done, but tried to catch some of the smaller ones, which were disappearing into the bushes. The boy smiled because that was what he always did when he was spoken to gently, as the man behind the wheel was doing now. He smiled because he was unable to speak; he never spoke a single word, or ever heard any: he didn't know what words were, although he knew they existed, that it was through them that adults and others the same size as him expressed what they wanted and expected of him, as long as they pointed to him, or showed him.

The man at the wheel got out, opened the rear door and signalled for him to enter.

The boy did so, struggling to clamber up into the car. He sat with his short legs on the seat and his feet dangling down, careful not to get anything dirty. He took off his black and green backpack, covered with stickers of cartoon characters he had never seen. He laid it beside him, took out a notebook and some coloured pencils, and began to draw. He couldn't write or read, and would never learn to do so, but he didn't know this, and thought that what he was doing was studying and so he did it conscientiously, drawing lines and shapes up and down, at the sides, making lines longer, rubbing some out, redoing the shapes, using another colour here and there, methodically and carefully completing scribbles that made no sense to anyone else.

The driver set off, slowly leaving behind the crowd of mothers and children hurrying towards the bus stops. The cracked pavements around the school were filled with narrow stores, a stationer's with a cluttered window display, a couple of grocers, a Korean trinkets shop, a laundry.

Peering in the rear-view mirror, the driver saw with amazement how quickly the boy had become absorbed in his own world.

He thought of himself at that age, running through the unpaved streets and constantly evolving houses in the shanty town on the city outskirts, which flooded whenever there was heavy rain. Shouting all the time, flying kites or delivering the lunch tins his grandmother cooked in her dark kitchen, up and down the *favela* he didn't even know was called that – to him it was simply the place his mother had brought him to and left him – a boy weighed down with lunch boxes, always shouting, shooing away the mongrels or calling to the customers, dodging and excusing himself to everybody in the alleyways because he was in a hurry to deliver the food, then fetch some more and deliver that too, and so on and on, until it was time to go to the school down the hill. Unable to sit still, he never took any interest in what the teachers were saying, but even so he listened and wrote down numbers and names, desperate to get out again and run home through the maze of shacks and cramped stores, although he didn't realize they were tiny and cramped because he had never known anything different and because he had never been taken outside that neighbourhood. Until one day his mother did so, accompanied this time by a man he had never seen before, a man who beat him so that he would be quiet and stop shouting and laughing and running round the gardens of the big house where his mother and the man worked.

Then one day, without deciding to, he fell silent. He became a quiet boy, a quiet youth, a quiet soldier, the quietest among the military police recruits, a quiet corporal out on patrol, a quiet sergeant during the raids on drug dens, a quiet patient while he was recovering from the bullet wound that shattered his knee, a quiet retired soldier in his bare city-centre apartment, a silent security driver whom the other employees looked up to and called the Major, a rank he had never reached.

He didn't feel sorry for the boy. He didn't particularly like the boy. He didn't particularly like anyone. Except for his daughter. Liking people, things, tastes, or whatever it might be, was not something that interested him. He was indifferent to others. To all others.

At least that was what he had convinced himself.

Normally he would not have picked the boy up. The VW hired to transport the children of the domestic employees in Jardim Paulistano was supposed to do that. He had already done his job earlier, when he took home the chubby boy who was as dark-skinned as his father, the owner of the car he was now driving. But the boss's wife gave the order. In this case, an unusual order, as unusual as the day had been so far. As unusual as his feeling had been when he saw the housekeepers' son at the school gate, pack on his back, so blond and pale-looking, so small, so . . . defenceless.

He followed the same route back as he had taken with the boss's kid.

It didn't take him long to reach Avenida Rebouças, with its usual annoying traffic. Switching on the radio, he heard the same news that had been in all the media since the start of that month: the Iraqi dictator had invaded Kuwait. With 60,000 soldiers, Saddam Hussein had seized a fifth of the world's oil reserves. The driver changed station, but eventually gave up and switched the radio off, fed up with the same blah-blah, the recession brought on by the Collor government impounding all bank deposits, even savings accounts, with more than 50,000 cruzeiros in them. He loathed politics, the commentators irritated him, he didn't much care for any kind of music, there was no football game on at that time of day. He preferred silence.

A few blocks further on, he turned right into Rua Joaquim Antunes. This was the start of a neighbourhood with tree-lined streets and quite elegant houses, built in one of the first waves of urban development which, in the second decade of the twentieth century, displaced affluent families from São Paulo to what had once been small farms to the west of the city.

The streets were quiet; nobody was walking on the pavements. The people living in this area travelled around only by car. The stream of vehicles trying to avoid rush-hour traffic jams would only start later in the afternoon.

He drove on slowly, taking the roundabouts carefully so that the German car's soft suspension did not sway too much and spoil the boy's concentration.

He looked at him again in the rear-view mirror. For

a split second, without realizing it, he was envious of him.

Happiness is easy. All you need is a piece of paper and a box of coloured pencils, he thought – almost at the same instant as the first bullet hit him.

His trained eye and brain immediately registered: a tall, hooded man in a dark-coloured parka, firing a long-barrelled Magnum with his left hand. He had jumped out of a black pick-up that had just blocked the path of the Mercedes-Benz. Two smaller cars were preventing any possible retreat backwards, and beyond them was a black saloon car. Other hooded figures were leaping out of the two smaller vehicles, running in his direction: one, two, three, four, five men, revolvers and pistols in their hands, none of them armed with anything more powerful. What are they doing, what do they want, he wondered, his right shoulder burning from the bullet that had whizzed through it. He put his weight on his left leg, straightening up and turning towards the back seat where the boy had stopped drawing and was peering at him quizzically, not comprehending what was going on. Shouting at the boy, forgetting he couldn't hear a thing, shouting for him to get down, to lie flat on the floor of the car, at the same time as he sees the hooded men coming towards him, only one of them firing – the one who has the silver Magnum in his left hand, the big guy who came out of the black pick-up, it must be him, it has to be him, but the boy doesn't move and the Major cannot reach him. He feels the impact of another bullet, this time in his left shoulder, it must be a crack shot who does not intend to kill him, if not he would have gone for the head, he had a clear enough sight for that, the Major reasons, leaning back still further but only succeeding in grabbing hold of the green and black backpack covered in cartoon stickers. Two hooded men open the rear doors of the Mercedes as he drops back into the front seat, reaching behind him for the Glock semi-automatic he keeps hidden under the seat, cursing himself for not doing this before, instead of trying to save the boy first, but the man in the dark parka is already alongside him, and quickly fires his .357 Magnum three times into his chest and the back of his head.

The boy is dragged out by the men from the smaller cars. They cover him with a sack, and pass him on to the driver of the pick-up, who carries him over to it and pushes him into the boot.

The giant with the long-barrelled Magnum .357 tosses a piece of paper on to the Major's lifeless body. On it are written two long numbers. An arrow, drawn with a fountain pen, points from the first series of numbers to the second. On the other side of the paper, written with the same pen: We have your son.

The black saloon, specially adapted for invalids, and the two smaller cars turn tail and speed off along the road they came in on, exactly forty-two seconds earlier. At the first roundabout, they head off in different directions. The other men pile into the pick-up, which drives off down the street opposite.

The big blue German car is the only vehicle left in the empty street.

The coloured pencils lie scattered on the asphalt around it.

2

EVEN SONS OF bitches can be moved, concluded Olavo Guaimiaba Bettencourt when he saw the eyes of the chairman of the state electricity company brimming with tears as the lights went up and the curtains were drawn back in the glass boardroom looking out over Avenue Cidade Jardim. It was the end of the showing of the short films filled with the testimonies of grateful inhabitants from the areas benefiting from new electricity networks, thanks to the hydro-electric power generated by the waters of the lakes that had drowned their farms and towns. In the most heart-rending of all, which he himself had directed, a wrinkled peasant woman spoke of how her son had died because of the lack of an incubator like the one recently installed in the clinic in the neighbouring village, and how under the electric light at the night school she had realized a dream of almost sixty years: to learn to read and write, as she did on the sign she held up for the camera, with four words scrawled on it: *Thank You, Mister President.*

Everyone applauded, following the lead of the state electricity company's media assessor. Ernesto Passeri, the man responsible for proposing that the advertising agency run by Olavo should tender for the generous publicity account, smiled and showed his brilliant white teeth, perfectly capped by the most expensive dentist in Brazil. He was genuinely pleased. Not because of the positive response to the campaign, which would have been approved anyway, but because of the whole slew of benefits that it would bring from now on – with him, by him, through him.

It was this man in his pinstripe suits made to measure in London and his Hermès ties who was responsible for measuring and tailoring the negotiations over the percentages of the campaign expenses that were to be diverted into the personal accounts of the president and the minister, and his own account, all held in Caribbean tax havens. A media campaign was planned that would guarantee whole pages in newspapers and magazines throughout Brazil, sixty-second TV adverts in the breaks during the most popular news programme and the eight o'clock soap opera, announcements in prestigious publications throughout the world that had not yet been finally selected but would doubtless include the *New York Times*, *The Times* of London, *Le Monde*, *Der Spiegel*, *El País*, *Clarín*, and possibly, the minister's long-held dream, a double-page spread in *Time* magazine itself. It was the moment to create a good international image for the government led by the young, good-looking Brazilian president, and all the important deals that could come out of it. Although it would be easier to receive undeclared percentages from deals made with Asian countries and industrialists. But there was time enough for that. A couple of years, perhaps a little more.

It didn't make much difference. The president who had taken office five months earlier was enjoying the highest popularity ratings since the days of Getúlio Vargas in the 1940s, the opposition was at sixes and sevens, in no time at all the re-election would be a shoo-in, as one of the most celebrated TV commentators liked to repeat in his daily stream of clichés. All those who counted had been bought. The percentages for the cheapskates in the advertising agencies and media companies – six per cent here, seven there, eleven later on, fifteen for those with the major accounts, were already accumulating in the tax havens. What was urgent now was the purchase of the new apartment in Manhattan.

Still applauding, Ernesto Passeri stood up and walked round to the other side of the marble-topped Saarinen table towards Olavo Bettencourt. His associate was as corpulent as his Tupinambá ancestors in the state of Pará, but preferred to sign using only his French surname and still had the smile of false modesty that Ernesto recognized from the days when they were both just starting out in their profession. Back then they were in charge of the account for a supermarket chain owned by the arrogant sons of a semi-literate Portuguese immigrant who had become a millionaire in less than ten years thanks to inflation and a complete lack of scruples. Ernesto and Olavo used to keep the three boys happy with luxury watches, holidays in ski resorts and the company of former beauty queens and soap-opera actresses (discreetly in the case of the two older sons, quite openly with the youngest, who was dazzled by having his photo in celebrity magazines). He himself looked after old man Liborio Freitas, forced to listen

18

hour after hour to the same stories about the adolescent from Póvoa do Varzim who disembarked in the port of Santos carrying only a woven bag and a scrap of paper with the address of an uncle in São Paulo whom he never located, and so found himself having to make his own way in the new country.

The old man and he developed almost an affection for each other, or at least a habit that filled the empty hours of this wealthy immigrant sneered at by his own sons. So much so that one day Freitas, almost as if he were delivering goods, presented him with his shy, apparently not very bright only daughter, Adélia. Ernesto married her, and she turned out to be astute enough to sideline her brothers when the business expanded, even before her father died, and which now included a chain of cheap clothing stores, another of furniture and household goods, and a recent partnership with Spanish businessmen interested in building hotels to bring mass tourism to the cities of Brazil's north-east. Adélia and he had not invested a cent of their own money in this venture: he was already part of the recently elected government, and the connections that had helped him rise through the bureaucracy had been well rewarded.

Still clasping Olavo's hand and bestowing gushing praise on him for films and adverts he himself had directed, Ernesto tried to steer him to the far side of the room. Olavo pretended not to understand what his agency's secret associate was trying to do. Instead, leaning over to the president of the state electricity company sitting beside him, he invited him to lunch at a steak restaurant on Rua Haddock Lobo that was always filled with faces and names he was bound to recognize and be pleased to mention when he was back in Brasília. The ex-senator, defeated along with all the other candidates from his party in the state elections, thought this was an excellent idea, and quickly dismissed the group accompanying him.

Ernesto stayed.

The chairman said, in a smug voice: 'I need a pee.' Olavo led him to the bathroom door. It was only when it was closed again that he said, without turning back towards Ernesto:

'No.'

'No, what? I haven't said a word, or asked you for anything.'

'No, Ernesto.'

'You haven't even heard what I have to say, and you're already saying no.'

'Precisely.'

'It's not for me, as you well know.'

'I know. And the answer's still no.'

'You're saying no to the minister, not to me.'

'I can't accept that request.'

'I haven't made the request yet. And it isn't really one.'

'It's a request, and it's about the accounts. I can't open yet another account abroad. There's no way I can justify it to the IRS.'

'The heiress?'

'The IRS: the Internal Revenue Service. The tough guys of US taxes.'

'Since when were you bothered about American taxation?'

'I sign the monthly cheques to pay for his daughter's studies at Stanford, for his son's film course at New York

University, their credit card bills, their rent, their trips. What if the IRS discovers that the money to pay for all this is deposited each month into my account by banks in the Caribbean?'

'That will never happen.'

'What if somebody in the Brazilian press finds out?'

'The journalists respect the minister.'

'Until the day they grow tired of the fairy tale about the poor boy who emerged from the jungle to become the most brilliant professor at São Paulo University. The minister's going on another trip to New York, isn't he? He's accompanying the president to the opening of the sessions at the United Nations. And then to the big banquet in his honour, isn't that right?'

Ernesto nodded.

'The whole of the Brazilian press will have its eye on him, on what he does, what he eats, where he goes, who he goes with, the meetings with his children.'

'But you don't know what the minister wants. You don't know what he needs you to do.'

'Is it a request or a threat?'

'Olavo, I don't think I need remind you of your own interests and those of your business.'

'Agency, Ernesto. Businesses have to do with industry, and I'm a man who creates.'

'If you say so. What the minister wants is for you . . .'

'Not now.'

'Now. Today or, at the latest, tomorrow.'

'There's a complication.'

'Personal or professional?'

'Personal.'

'We can talk about that some other time. What the minister wants is for you to pay for an apartment he liked in Central Park South. Next to the Plaza Hotel.'

'Perfect for him to go in and out of without being seen when he's meeting investors or lovers.'

'That's not your concern or mine. The ideal would be for you to travel to New York tonight.'

'Tonight is impossible. Don't even think it. I can't leave the agency from one hour to the next.'

'Tomorrow then. I've already bought two tickets. First class, of course. Take your wife. Go with Mara, put a credit card in her hand, take her to see a Broadway musical, make it look like a little pleasure trip. The apartment will be paid for in cash.'

'In real money? Are you all crazy? Remember, Al Capone was only put in jail because he tried to dodge income tax.'

'You're not Al Capone, and we're not gangsters. We're simply public-spirited businessmen with sound plans to turn Brazil into a first-world country. You're to use the money deposited each month in your account with that Israeli bank. The FBI turns a blind eye to it because they also use it when necessary. In all its forty-year existence, none of its clients has ever had any problem.'

Ernesto held out a business card.

'This is the estate agent.'

Olavo took the card, glanced at it, and said:

'A Brazilian.'

'Cuban. But he changed the Z at the end of the name to an

22

S to look more Brazilian. He's been doing business with Brazilians and Portuguese since the seventies.'

The sound of the toilet door being unlocked silenced them. The chairman of the state electricity company came out, still wiping his hands on a light-blue linen handkerchief. Olavo wondered why he hadn't used one of the towels stacked on the washbasin. And what kind of person still went around carrying a linen handkerchief.

3

Monday 20 August, 07.12

I'M NOT HAPPY with you, she rehearsed yet again, eyes shut, her back towards the bathroom from where came the sounds of Olavo's annoyingly interminable shower. Typical of an Indian, she thought, yet again, yet another morning, five years after she had announced she was pregnant and he had separated from the woman he had married before his social and economic rise as the head of the most creative and award-winning advertising agency of the past decade. But I can't simply say I'm Not Happy With You. That's going to annoy him as much as if I was confessing I had a lover. Better to turn things the other way round. Transfer the dissatisfaction. Olavo, You Are Not Happy With Me. Or possibly, Olavo, I Don't Make You Happy. No, I can't put it to him like that, it won't work. He *is* happy with me. I make him happy. I'm everything he ever dreamed of. More. I'm what he never imagined he could have. I'm the one who can't bear this any more.

I can't bear this fat man snorting on top of me, sticking that long thing of his in me, giving me stomach ache and always expecting me to go: oh, Olavo, ah Olavo, oh yes, oh yes, oh yes Olavo, Olavo, Olavo, come Olavo! He comes. It's not worth it. It's a very high price to pay for this house in Jardim Paulistano, for these four-hundred-thread Egyptian cotton sheets, the Versace dresses, the gold Rolex, for the beach house in Maresias, my mother's apartment in Porto Alegre, for the Mercedes-Benz with a driver, the six servants, the flights in first class, the ski holidays in Aspen, the limitless spending in Miami, dinners in Paris, the apartment on 72nd Street in Manhattan. It's not worth it. They're not worth it.

She opened her eyes. On the bedside table, next to the Italian lamp, stood a black-and-white photograph in a silver frame bought in the same store as in the film where Audrey Hepburn sang that song and ate a hotdog staring into its windows on her way back from a date with a client. That was where Olavo bought her first diamond ring, before they were married. Olavo chose the photograph, arguing that black and white was more chic; it showed the three of them, her, Olavo and their son Olavinho (Olavo chose that name too, she preferred Rodrigo, William or Leonardo). The three of them were sitting on an antique-looking sofa; she was wearing a Chanel-type fitted dress, but sexier, also by Versace, but bought in Bloomingdale's. Her husband was sitting stiffly on her right, her son on her left. Both of them were smiling; she had only the faint hint of a smile on her lips as the three of them stared straight at the camera.

She closed her eyes again.

She hated that photograph.

My god, that slob of a child. I'm the mother of that. Of that dark-skinned, almost teak-coloured boy, darker even than his father, with those flabby cheeks and that needy look of his. He needs me all the time, he wants me to feel sorry for him, to hold him, stroke him, to kiss him, he wants me to hug him, cuddle him, pay attention to what he says, join in his games, look at any bit of paper he's scrawled some stupid drawing on, play with yet another superhero figure he's been given by his father, listen to his stories about what he's learned at school, what some little friend of his has said, the knee he scraped when he fell, oh my god, always begging, always snivelling, oh how dreadful. How dreadful!

No. No, I mustn't think that. I can't feel that. I can't be disgusted by my own son, I can't, I can't. I must love my son. I must. All mothers love their sons, I love my son, I love my son, I'm not disgusted by my son, I feel love for my son, love, love, love. I love my son. I love my son. I love my little Indian son. My little Indian son who's as fat and oily as his father, greasy like his father, exactly like his father, curl for curl of his thick black hair, greasy skin for greasy skin, flat feet for flat feet, knock-knees for knock-knees, soft belly for soft belly, spaced-out teeth for spaced-out teeth, bulbous nose for bulbous nose. I'm not disgusted by my son. I'm not. I can't be. I'm not. I love my son. I love him. Do I?

The sound of the shower came to an end.

Now he's going to shave, thought Mara. He's going to take between two and five minutes to spread the foam on his flabby cheeks, wait for the sparse Indian bristles to soften, then shave them off. Afterwards he'll dab on one of the many French aftershaves bought with perfumes in the duty-free shop at Paris airport and scattered on the shelf above the washbasin, all of them smelling too strong, and use the roll-on deodorant he buys by the dozen in that pharmacy near our apartment on 72nd Street. And before long he'll open that door, naked, already half aroused, he'll come over here, pull back the sheets covering me, lift my nightdress and push himself against me. Exactly the way he is doing now. And he'll say, as he is doing:

'Mara . . . Mara . . .'

I'll pretend I'm just waking up, I'll moan, knowing that excites him still further. He'll repeat:

'Mara . . . Mara . . .'

I'll groan again, turning my body a little towards him, feeling his prick pulsating between my backside and my thighs, which I'll open just a little. I'll groan again, still with my eyes closed. I'll mutter something, rubbing my back against his chest and stomach.

'Mara, Mara,' he'll go on saying, as one of his hands comes round to squeeze my breasts, and he thrusts his fat thighs between mine.

'Mmm . . . ah . . . mmm.' I'll say something like that, like a woman waking up to the caresses of the husband she loves is supposed to do. Perhaps I'll say his name, yes, good idea, I'll say his name sighing a little, pretending I'm taken by surprise. 'Olavo . . . mmm . . . ah . . . What are you up to, ah . . . mmm . . . Olavo?'

'My love . . .' Generally this is when he starts to call me My Love; 'My love, I adore you,' he'll say, as he is doing now, kissing my neck, drooling with his rough tongue rather than kissing, and lifting the nightdress up to my midriff.

This is when I lie completely still, to allow him to take my night things off without getting them torn or frayed, as has happened on several occasions. I don't say a word. I simply sigh a little louder and roll my blue eyes, half opening my lips, which he presses against his, sticking his darting, hard tongue into my mouth and pushing it around. It still has the minty taste of his anti-caries American toothpaste on it.

He rolls his body on top of mine.

He brings his face up against me, flattens my nose, smears his minty saliva all over me.

He's very heavy.

I can't breathe properly.

I'll escape by sitting on top of him, I'll push my long blonde hair to one side, rub my breasts against his chest.

My love, my love, you drive me crazy, he will say, or something similar. And I . . . And I . . .

Mara suddenly straightens up, jumps off the bed and runs to the bathroom, saying Just a Second, Darling, I'll Be Quick, Just a Second . . .

She shuts the door.

She scarcely has time to reach the bowl. She vomits into water that is already yellow from Olavo's urine: he never flushes the toilet. She goes over to the washbasin, rinses her face. Tears start to flow, she can't stop them. She rinses her face again. Breathes deeply, once, twice, three, four times. The tears dry up. The shame she feels does not.

She opens the bathroom cabinet, takes out the tube of vaginal jelly, unscrews it, presses it between her fingers (it's almost finished, she must remember to buy some more), lubricates herself.

She washes her hands, dries them, fluffs up her hair.

She smiles at herself in the mirror, the most sincerely pleased and excited smile she can muster. Not good enough. She tries again. Better.

Another deep breath.

She flushes the toilet, until all traces of urine and vomit disappear.

She opens the bathroom door. Her features, a captivating mixture of genes of immigrants from the Azores, Holstein and Piedmont, are picked out by the morning light filtering through the wooden shutters. She tells the man in the king-size bed to stroke his penis, in exactly the same way she has told many others lying waiting for her on hotel or motel beds when her visiting card still declared that she was a model, in the days when she lived on the air shuttle between Porto Alegre–São Paulo–Rio de Janeiro as an executive escort, and said her name was Pamela or Vanessa or Claudia or Isadora.

I'm ready for you now, my love.

4

IRENE BAUER SPREAD the manioc flour in the hot frying pan without even a drop of fat, the way Doctor Olavo liked it and had taught her to do. She knew how to make her employers appreciate her. She learned rapidly how to make a perfect pancake, even though she had never seen one before. Saucepans, ovens, frying pans, nothing in a kitchen or house held any secret for her. She was a quick learner; since her childhood in the interior of the southern state of Santa Catarina she could cook anything as soon as she was shown how, or given a recipe. She knew how to read and add up very well, perhaps even better than her husband, Stephan. That's why, from the moment she started school in Anitápolis, she was entrusted with looking after the accounts for her parents' farm, then of her own home on the outskirts of the nearby city of Santa Rosa de Lima. The same was true here, where she and Stephan were the housekeepers, and would be for possibly another ten or twelve years, until they had saved enough to return to the cascades, pine woods and green hills of southern Brazil that she missed so badly.

The pancake came unstuck from the frying pan. It was ready.

Irene slid it on to a plate, filled it with dried beef and cream, sprinkled on some sesame seeds, and took it over to Doctor Olavo. He was seated at the breakfast table, on which stood imported jams and others that she made but he never tried. No milk, no juice, no fruit, no yoghurt, no fresh curds, no toast, no wholemeal bread, no baguette, no banana fritters, no orange cake, nothing: just black coffee and pancakes. He wanted the table laid with all these tokens of abundance, but pancakes and black coffee were all he ever had for breakfast. The only thing that changed was the filling.

'Shall I make some more, Doctor?'

He took his breakfast alone. He did not talk. He leafed through the newspapers, and occasionally got up to watch an item that might interest him on the TV news. Irene noticed this always had to do with politics. Or Formula One. And tennis matches as well.

'Good idea. Do we have any caramel jam?'

His wife only came down later in the morning. She had a natural yoghurt with granola, a piece of fruit, drank a small coffee, and that was that. She was always on a diet. She was the only woman from Rio Grande do Sul in the south of Brazil who didn't like maté tea. She thought it was common. And she didn't like to remember what her origins were.

'Yes, we do. And we've also got some of that sweet they brought from the north for you.'

'Cupuaçu?'

'That's it. It's on the table there. Next to the tangerine jam.'

She stepped forward, picked up both pots, put them closer to her boss, then went back to the stove. The frying pan was at the ideal temperature now. She sprinkled the greyish flour into it.

Doctor Olavo and Dona Mara's son had already had breakfast. Unlike in recent weeks, he wasn't able to wait to be taken to school by his father. He left earlier, with his mother's driver and a guard, to rehearse something for a party being organized for the British consul. Irene knew his school had some link with Princess Diana's country. Olavinho learned everything in English, his lessons, arithmetic, everything. That was how he was taught in his school, and it was that language his father used to talk to him, when he had time, because he had so little of it, he was always working, travelling to Brasília or the United States, or going to banquets and parties. Always. Olavinho was restless, unsettled, he ran about the house the whole time and talked a lot; he never stopped, always asking questions and never waiting for the replies. The opposite of the endless silence of her own son.

The fresh pancake was ready. Irene slid it on to another plate.

'Would you like me to fill it with caramel jam or the other one?'

'I can do that, Irene.'

Olavo stuck a silver Christofle spoon into the caramel jam, scooped up a generous amount, and spread it on the pancake.

'There's no need to make any more,' he said with his mouth full, and rising to his feet. 'Did my wife's driver return yet?'

'Not yet. But your driver is waiting.'

'After he drops me at the agency, my driver will be working with Doctor Ernesto, who's coming back from Brasília and has several meetings in places my driver knows well. Tell the Major I'll be needing him from six onwards. He's to put the car in the basement garage. And tell Dona Mara I'll be home for dinner.'

Irene nodded, and her employer left the room. Through the window she saw him go out to the armour-plated Mercedes-Benz and sit behind the driver. At that moment the gates were opened by the two armed men and a dark-blue car came in. It pulled up alongside the other one. Doctor Olavo rolled down the window, said something to the Major, then closed the window again. His car moved out of the gate. The Major got out of his car, walked over to the guard-post. Irene called out to him. He walked over slowly, with an almost imperceptible limp.

'Doctor Olavo left a message for . . .'

'I know,' he said roughly. An image of live electric wires went through Irene's mind. 'He gave me his instructions.'

'To pick him up at the . . .'

'Yes,' he said, then turned his back on her and continued on his way to the guard-post.

The very small, very blond boy sitting on the ground near the gate did not even seem to notice when the Major passed him by. His backpack was on the ground next to him. He was waiting to be taken to his special school. Irene would do that in a little while, as soon as she was free of her duties in the kitchen. She had finished putting away the jams and butter in the refrigerator when her boss's wife came in. She was wearing make-up and was dressed to go out. Irene was surprised: Dona Mara never came down before half-past nine or ten, which gave Irene just enough time to take the boy to school and return. This break in routine left her not knowing what to do. Hesitating, she took a yoghurt from the still-open refrigerator.

'I don't want any,' Mara said. 'I'm not going eat anything.'

'Not even a . . .?'

'Nothing, Irene. My little . . .'

'A pear? There's papaya. Melon.'

'Nothing. Has my little boy already gone to the English school with his father?'

'He went with the Major today. Wouldn't you like a coffee, Dona Mara?'

'What time did he leave?'

'At half-past six. Can I make you an espresso?'

'So early. Does he always leave at that time? Every day?'

'That used to be his timetable, but in recent weeks his father has been taking him later. I'll make an espresso. I just have to press here,' she said, switching on the De'Longhi coffee machine Olavo had bought in Milan.

'Does the boy cry? Or complain?'

'About waking up so early? No, ma'am. Would you like a piece of toast? I can make you one.'

'And the boy doesn't say anything?'

'He says a lot. As you know. He asks things, asks for you, for his father. He's very curious.'

'Call my driver. Does he know where the English School is?'

'The Major does, ma'am. He used to take him in the past.'

'The Major?'

'The driver. He was in the military police. He knows where the school is. The coffee will be ready in a minute.'

'The military police?'

'He's a security guard as well. Dom Olavo says he's the best.'

'That tall, thin guy?'

'Yes, Dona Mara. There are some biscuits too. Cream biscuits. I made them yesterday. I'll get you one. They go well with coffee.'

The blonde, made-up woman, wearing the dress and shoes she had bought recently in a three-floor boutique run by a dressmaker from Calabria on Fifth Avenue in Manhattan, looked out of the window. She saw a very white, very blond and very quiet little boy sitting on the ledge near the guard-post. For a moment she stood stock still. She felt a shiver go down her spine. She didn't know whether it was a premonition or the shock of realizing, for the first time, how extraordinarily beautiful the boy was.

'Your son . . .' She pointed to the boy.

'Yes, that's him, ma'am.'

'Your son is very quiet.'

'Yes he is, ma'am.'

'I've never heard him say anything.'

'No, ma'am.'

'He doesn't shout, he doesn't cry.'

'No, ma'am.'

'He . . .'

'He doesn't talk, no, ma'am.'

'Nothing? Ever?'

35

'He doesn't hear either.'

'He doesn't . . . ?'

'No, never.'

'But a child who's so . . .'

'He's not stupid, ma'am.'

'That's not what I was going to say.'

'Lots of people think he is slow because he doesn't talk or hear. But he isn't.'

'What's his name?'

'The coffee's ready. Would you like sugar or sweetener?'

Mara took the saccharin. She drank the espresso in two gulps. She liked hot things: coffees, teas, soups, even the maté tea she never wanted to taste again.

She opened her bag, searched in it, but couldn't find what she was looking for.

'Do you have any cigarettes, Irene?'

'I don't smoke, ma'am. Would you like me to send Stephan to buy a pack?'

'There's no need. One of the guards must have some. Go and get me one.'

While she was waiting, she walked aimlessly up and down the breakfast room. The table still showed tell-tale signs of her husband: the crumpled newspapers, with the economy supplement folded. The napkin tossed on to the chair. The cup with the remains of his coffee in it. The plate with the remains of a pancake still oozing caramel jam.

She went back to the window. The boy was still sitting in the same place, as immobile as before. Part of the driver's back was visible. He had taken off his jacket, and had a pistol stuck in the waistband of his trousers.

Irene came back. She brought a single cigarette, plus a lighter. Mara snatched them from her, lit the cigarette, took a long drag, blew out the smoke, then stubbed the cigarette out in the caramel jam dish.

'Tell the driver I want to leave now. I'm going to get Olavinho at the English School.'

'Now?'

'Now.'

'He has school till two in the afternoon.'

'I'm going to fetch my boy now. I'm going to take him to the mall, then we'll have lunch, then we're going to a movie. I want to spend the day with my son.'

Irene didn't move.

'Go on. Call the driver.'

'Dona Mara . . .' The housekeeper hesitated. 'The thing is . . . the Major . . .'

Irene was afraid of annoying her employer. Perhaps Dona Mara would think it was an abuse.

'The thing is that the Major normally, at this time of day . . . once he has dropped Olavinho at school and you don't need him yet, then the Major . . . I ask him to . . . It's something quick, so that I don't waste time on it . . . and seeing the car is already there . . .'

Mara waited for the stocky peasant woman to finish her explanation.

'. . . So that I am here when you come down for breakfast, the Major . . . to do everything more rapidly, because of all the traffic jams in this city, I . . . instead of going in the Combi or by bus . . . I ask him to . . .' Irene plucked up her courage, and finished everything in a rush. 'I ask him to take me and my boy to school in the car, to take both of us, my boy and I, but we sit in the front, we don't sit in the rear seat, I know that's for you and the master, we sit with the Major, alongside him, and now it's time for me to go with him, otherwise he'll miss his classes, and . . .'

'I'll take your boy in the car, Irene, and drop him at school. You can stay here. Go and call the driver.'

5

Previous week
Tuesday 14 August, 21.41

THE DOORBELL TO the bedsitter rang four times. Four short rings that roused him from his stupor in front of the television. The Major stood up and, with an automatic gesture, picked up his Glock 22 pistol from the table cluttered with beer cans, an empty pizza box and some videos he was always forgetting to return, and flicked the safety catch off.

'Who's there?'

'It's me, Dad,' replied a female voice that was low but still had a slight childish ring to it. 'I'm all alone. You can open up.'

The flat was tiny: he had only to stretch out his hand to undo the lock and the two bolts. Barbara came in, shutting the door behind her. The Major locked it and drew the bolts again.

'Do you need all that?' she asked, looking for somewhere to put her backpack. 'Why are you so paranoid?'

'Leave it here,' he said, pointing to the table, securing the pistol then slipping it into the waistband behind his back. He pushed away the videos, picked up the pizza box, folded it and took it to the sink beside the stove with two burners in the windowless cubicle the estate agents called a galley kitchen.

Barbara put the backpack down. She took off her navy-blue jacket and laid it on top. She straightened her blouse and her striped grey-and-blue sweater on her skinny body. She had inherited her tall, light-skinned look from her father, who in turn had inherited it from her grandfather, a ranch hand in the interior of Paraíba state, a distant mix of Dutch invaders and Angolan maids.

She was a gawky adolescent, lacking the lively, carefree attitude typical of many girls her age. The Major was worried she might end up as detached from life as him. But he didn't know how to avoid that. Or to talk about it.

'I'm thirsty. Do you have any Coke?'

'Water.'

'OK.'

The Major took one of the glasses from the sink, rinsed it, filled it from a plastic bottle of water that was already out of the refrigerator, and handed it to his daughter. She hardly took a mouthful. She wasn't really thirsty, but didn't know how to start this conversation with her father. She never knew how to start a conversation with him. She never knew how to start a conversation, purely and simply.

'You don't drink soft drinks, Father?'

He didn't remember her addressing him like that before, or perhaps it had happened without him noticing it. He liked it: children should treat their parents with respect. No, daughter, I don't drink soft drinks, it may be I don't like them, or it may even be that I do, I don't know, but I never got used to them.

In our house, in all the houses I've lived in, we only had soft drinks on feast days, sometimes on Sundays, or when a visitor brought some. In the barracks it was water or maté tea or orangeade served with our rations, and some other drink I don't remember, but water was good enough for me, it was all you needed to quench your thirst. He thought of saying all this, and yet he remained silent, standing in the doorway between the kitchen and the cramped area that was his living room.

Barbara was going to put the glass down on the table, but changed her mind. It was good to have something to hold on to, if you didn't really know what you were going to say, or how to say it.

'Father . . .' she began.

'What are you doing here at this time of day? And with that backpack?'

'My books. Revision, really.'

Barbara switched the glass to her other hand, took another mouthful. She used her free hand to push part of her untidy dark-brown hair behind her ear.

The Major studied all his daughter's gestures. If he were to interpret them according to the lessons he had learned at the police academy, he would say that the nervousness evident in this adolescent in jeans and trainers came not from what she wanted to say, but from what she wanted to leave out, so as not to compromise the others involved.

'I'm studying close to here.'

But he didn't want to listen to his daughter as if she were one of the many young girls who lived in the poor outskirts of

41

this inhospitable city. Even when he was still married to her mother, he hardly used to see Barbara, and since they had separated six years earlier he had seen her less and less. The fortnightly weekend visits that the judge had stipulated after his ex-wife had accused him of domestic violence rarely coincided with his Saturday or Sunday leave. And he didn't like Barbara coming to his flat. Almost all this central district was full of drug addicts, prostitutes and layabouts selling cocaine and weed. He had even had to throw a smartarse dealer out of his own building.

'I'm taking a course in . . .'

'Near here?'

'Two blocks away. Three. A bit more. Pre-university entrance. I want to try for the university entrance exam. It's a preparatory course for that. I mean, it's an English secretarial course, but it'll help me get a better job so that I can pay for the university entrance course. I want to take the exam.'

It's almost ten at night. The night courses and schools finish at around eight, eight-thirty, nine. The streets are poorly lit. A skinny girl like her would be an easy victim. Assault, rape, rape and murder. Barbara shouldn't be here.

'Why don't you study in your own neighbourhood?'

'There aren't any English classes in Barra Funda.'

'Everywhere has English classes. Every neighbourhood in São Paulo has some English classes.'

'But this is English for university entrance. We don't have that in Barra Funda. Not that kind of course. I want to take the exam for biology. Or chemistry. Or medicine. I need good English to get in. I don't know any English. I mean, I know a little, but not enough. To get in to study medicine it's not enough.'

'You said biology.'

'Bio-medical subjects. Biology, medicine, dentistry . . .'

'And how are you paying for your English course here in the centre?'

Barbara lowered her eyes, took another sip of water. She tried to look her father in the face, but found it impossible. She tried again, but ended up looking at the floor once more.

She doesn't want to lie, but she isn't telling me the truth either. She knows I know that her mother and stepfather had their savings seized by the government and won't be able to pay for this higher level course. The money I was putting aside for her studies has evaporated as well. The personal savings I've been putting aside ever since I was an army private have gone up in smoke, as is the case with thousands, possibly millions of other Brazilians. Now all I have is my pension, and that's being eaten away by inflation every month. This job I got two months ago as a driver and security guard isn't official, to avoid any problems with my disability pension. It pays next to nothing and I still haven't been able to give her mother or her anything.

'Who's going to pay?'

'Nobody, Father.'

'Somebody's paying. Somebody has to pay.'

'No one.'

'Who? A boyfriend?'

'I don't have a boyfriend.'

'Who then?'

'Father, you're not going to like it, but I had to do it.'

'To do what?'

'An exchange. I'm paying for the course by working in exchange.'

'What kind of exchange?'

'I work there in the school. And they let me study for nothing.'

'What work? What kind of work are you doing? You're only sixteen.'

'General duties.'

'What kind of general duties?'

'I tidy up a bit, do a little cleaning. That kind of work.'

It took the Major a few seconds to comprehend what his daughter was saying.

'That kind of work is what a cleaner does.'

'No, Father, I'm not a cleaner. Not exactly.'

'Daughter, you're working as a cleaner. Instead of studying, you're working as a cleaner.'

'It's only light work, Father. In the afternoons, and part of the night. In the morning, I take the course.'

'Does your mother know? Did she let you do it?'

'Yes, she knows. And she let me.'

'A cleaner . . . at sixteen.'

'It's more like removing any rubbish the students leave, wiping the blackboards clean, sweeping the classrooms. Not much at all. I don't have to clean the toilets, or anything like that.'

'But you're only sixteen.'

'I'll soon be seventeen. All the girls my age are working.'

'Are they cleaners too? All of them?'

'Some are shop assistants, others work in supermarkets: one of them is a cashier already. But none of them wants to study. None of them wants to get on. I do. I want to.'

'A person who cleans doesn't have time to study. I know, my mother was a cleaner. I don't want you to do that kind of work. You have to have time to study. I'm going to find a way to give you more money. I'll pay for your course. How much does that English course cost? Tell me how much. I'll get the money.'

Barbara put the glass on the crowded table. She wanted to cry. She knew her father was being sincere, but she also knew there was no way he could fulfil his promise. She bit her lip. She wanted to go over and give him a hug. But they weren't the kind of father and daughter who embraced, and so she didn't move.

'Father, look at your flat. You don't have anything. You've got your bed, that sofa, an old TV, and a videocassette player that's older still. That's it. Nothing more. You don't even have a dining table. You have no car, no telephone, no sound system or colour TV, nothing, Dad. Nothing.'

'There's a telephone at my new job. There are telephones in the street. I don't listen to music, and I watch any old rubbish on TV. I don't need any of that. I don't need anything. Here . . .' He gave her a piece of paper from the cigarette packet, on which he had written a phone number. 'Ring this number if you need to.'

She put the piece of paper away in one of the pockets of her backpack, knowing she would never call him at his

45

boss's home, and that he would never use the phone either.

'How much does that English course cost?'

'Nothing. It doesn't cost anything, Dad. They gave me a grant. I've been working there for a week. Don't worry about me. Do something for yourself, Dad. You give me all the money you get. You always have. But now we're poor, Dad. You, me, my mother, everybody I know is poor. You had to take on that job as a driver. Mother's hairdressing salon is always empty. Nobody has the money any more to have their nails done, or to pay to have their hair dyed or straightened, nothing. Nobody ever goes into the car-parts store my step-father runs. Nobody is buying anything. Nobody can buy anything. Nobody has any money for anything. Nothing, Dad. Nothing. We're all poor. There's no way out. This job will give me the chance to study. I'm not going to get very tired. It's light work. I'm going to do it, Dad. I am.'

6

WHEN MARA GOT into the car, the air-conditioning was already on at full blast, as she always instructed the drivers. It was sufficiently cool not to spoil her carefully applied make-up. She never left her bedroom without composing the face she wanted to present to the world. The Major had already been informed of where they were going.

A guard closed the Mercedes-Benz door. Standing on the lawn beside the garage, Irene watched this activity with the same inscrutable expression she wore all day long, wherever she was in the house. The boy wasn't with her, or in the car, apparently. Before Mara could ask what had happened to the housekeepers' son she was going to drop off at his special school, she caught sight of the top of his very blond head on the seat next to the driver. How small he is, she thought. How old can he be?

They pulled out into the street. The gates swung shut behind them. She saw the sun flickering through the leaves of the trees, the splashes of light on the asphalt. A fine August day which reminded her of the month of May in the south of

Brazil. Then she again saw the top – just the top – of the blond head in front of her.

'Why is the boy sitting in the front seat?'

'They always travel in the front. Irene . . . Dona Irene,' said the Major, correcting himself, 'knows that employees don't travel in the back seats.'

'But children should be in the back,' she said, trying to sound sensible and maternal. 'Put the child here.'

'He's used to travelling in the front, Dona Mara.'

'Put him back here,' she repeated, sure she was doing something laudable.

'Right now?'

'Yes, of course.'

The Major signalled; he wanted to do a U-turn then and there, but at that moment a grey Beetle appeared in his rear-view mirror. He waited.

'What are you doing?'

'I'm going back to the house so I can move him.'

'Why?'

'We're close by. It won't take a minute.'

'Stop here and bring the boy round.'

'I can't. We have orders not to let you or any other passenger out of the car.'

'Rubbish. Stop here.'

'We have instructions that say we should not—'

'Stop the car, Major. Then put the boy in the back.'

He obeyed reluctantly. He drew up by the kerb. The grey Beetle passed them. The Major got out and walked round the front of the car, irritated. He did not notice that the Beetle had pulled up on the next corner, its engine still running.

He opened the Mercedes-Benz door, undid the boy's seat-belt, picked him up under the arms and lifted him out of the seat. The boy began to kick his legs and wriggle. He was pointing insistently at something. His backpack, which was still on the seat.

The Major set him down. He bent to get the backpack at the same time as an impatient Mara opened the door on her side. She stepped out of the car and took hold of the child's hand, trying to get him in. He didn't seem to understand. Then she picked him up, surprised at how light he seemed. At exactly the same moment, a mustard-coloured Fiat passed them, heading slowly in the opposite direction.

The boy let himself be taken into the back of the car without protesting. The oval-faced man with curly hair driving the Fiat noted what seemed to him like a warm, maternal gesture, and the similarity between the blonde-haired, light-skinned woman and the blond, pale-skinned boy.

Depositing the backpack on the floor in front of the boy, the Major shut the rear door, went back to the driving seat and set off again.

The boy was staring at Mara. There was no expression on his face, not even curiosity about this woman who had lifted him up, or satisfaction at being free of the seat-belt. Even so, he was trying to place this smiling face in the sequence of those registered in his memory, although they never stayed there for long. He was pleased to be sitting without a belt on this back seat, and liked her sweet smell.

His fixed gaze disturbed Mara. She felt she was being

scrutinized. She turned towards the boy with a frown that she hoped would discourage him, but was taken aback by her own sense of shock: he's so small, she realized again. How old could he be?

'How old is this boy?' she asked the Major.

'I don't know, Dona Mara.'

'Three? Four? Five?'

'I don't know, Dona Mara.'

'Didn't his parents tell you?'

'They don't talk about him.'

'Is he dumb?'

'Yes.'

'Deaf as well?'

'Yes.'

Mara crossed her legs, taking care not to crumple her skirt or show her thighs. She opened her bag, searching for a cigarette. The gold Dupont lighter Olavo had given her was there, but no cigarette pack.

'Do you have any cigarettes, Major?'

'Yes, but . . .'

Mara lifted her arm towards the driver before he could finish his sentence: it was an order, not a request.

'. . . they're very strong.'

Her hand was stretched out, the first and middle fingers close to his shoulder. The Major took a red-and-white pack out of the pocket of his synthetic black jacket and held it up for her.

'Are these any good?'

'It's all the same to me.'

The boy followed her gesture of fishing out a cigarette, putting it between her lips and taking out the lighter. But she didn't light it. Something was inhibiting her, although she didn't know what. It didn't matter. She would smoke after they had dropped off the child, before she picked up Olavinho. She clasped the cigarette between her fingers.

'Does the boy always stare at people like that?'

'That or drawing.'

How unpleasantly insistent, she thought. But why does it make me feel so awkward? He's no more than a child. Yet it does make me feel awkward. And there's no point telling him to stop staring at me like that, he wouldn't hear.

'Will it take long to get to his school?'

'About twenty minutes, Dona Mara.'

There were too many cars on the streets and avenues of São Paulo, she thought. She was always arriving late. She found it impossible to calculate how long it would take her to get from one place to another. Was she going to have to put up with the boy staring at her for another twenty minutes?

'As long as that? Is the traffic bad again?'

'It's normal.'

Normal for people from São Paulo, she thought, these slow queues of traffic. And it's barely nine in the morning. Nineforty. Perhaps it wasn't a good idea getting the boy to sit next to me. Perhaps I should have left him sitting on the front seat. That's what he's used to. That's what he does when he goes to school with his mother. When the Major takes them. Employees and their children don't sit in the back seats. I know that, I only need to remind myself. He's not used to sitting here. He probably doesn't understand. That's why he keeps staring at me. I am his mother's boss. He must realize that, in some way. Even though he is so small: how old can he be? I shouldn't have yielded to my impulse. Something always goes wrong when I give in to my impulses. I should have let him stay where he was. Then I wouldn't feel as I do now. As if I was the intruder, not him. As if this is where he belongs, and I was the one brought here from the front seat. That blond hair of his. So blond it looks white. And so fine. So fine. I bet that if I blew on it, it would—

'There's some paper and pencils in his backpack.'

'What's that?'

'In his backpack.'

She realized the Major was suggesting a way to divert the boy's attention. Forgetting the way he made her feel, she bent over – keeping her legs close together and moving them to one side in the elegant manner she had learned when she was a beauty queen contestant in her native city – and undid the zip on the rubber-finished backpack covered in stickers of Walt Disney cartoon characters. Plunging in her manicured hand, she pulled out what she thought must be his notebooks. They were ugly, greyish, the cheapest paper. They had a smell that possibly other people would not have perceived, but which she did: the vague sour smell of paste, like a cloth dirty with vomit that has not been properly washed. The smell of her own schoolbooks, from the state school in Tramandaí where her mother left her every morning before she went off to clean and cook in other people's houses. Before they had moved to the state capital.

She felt a light hand on her arm. She turned to look. The boy's tiny hand slid into hers, and seemed to squeeze it, seemed to be giving her a . . . caress?

He cocked his head to one side and started to smile.

Mara handed him the notebooks, then bent down again. She found some coloured pencils, and put them on the seat between them. The boy chose a green one and started to draw, immediately absorbed in his task.

7

HE WATCHED FROM inside the Monza from the moment the man came out of the house squeezed in between similarly nondescript houses, on the side of the street with no pavement. A single mercury streetlamp spread a bluish glow over the potholed asphalt. The man was energetically pushing the bicycle wheels fitted to his invalid's chair. He never used crutches. He sped along without difficulty. He had the strength and size of his Visigoth ancestors from the north of Portugal mixed with the survivors of the trade in black slave ships, complemented by muscles worked on with weights and machines since his days as an adolescent in the sixties, back in the interior of Rio de Janeiro state.

He headed straight for the car, opened the door, pressed down on the arms of the wheelchair, and swung in alongside the driver. They did not greet each other. He folded the wheelchair and put it on the back seat. Then he told his curly-haired companion to drive straight on.

'Where to?' asked the driver, in Spanish with a Chilean accent.

'Straight on, just drive. We can't stay around here,' said Antonio, then fell quiet.

They drove on in silence until they had left behind the mean streets of the Sacomã district.

'What did you find out?' asked the Chilean.

'He's moved.'

'Where to? Why? Where's he gone?'

'Not so quickly, I can hardly understand your Spanish.'

'Where's he moving to?' insisted the Chilean anxiously. 'Why is he moving?'

'He's already moved. He left his house in Alphaville and has gone to live in a district with richer people.'

'Where? What *barrio*?'

'In Portuguese we say *bairro*.'

'When?'

'Last weekend. He moved to a house in Jardim Paulistano.'

'But why? Just like that, from one moment to the next?'

'Nobody could tell me. No one knew he was going to leave Alphaville. He dismissed his staff on Thursday. He paid their wages until the end of the year. He took lots of boxes with him. A removals company organized everything in a day. By Saturday he was no longer in the apartment. They say he bought the new house and all its contents.'

'All its contents?'

'With all the furniture and everything. The previous owners' housekeepers stayed on.'

'Nobody buys a house like that, all of a sudden.'

'I wish you wouldn't speak your Chilean Spanish so quickly.'

'Nobody buys . . .'

'I understood. But I don't like your language. Or your country.'

'I don't like what's become of my country these days either,' the Chilean retorted.

Chile is falling apart, he reflected. Since he took office in March, Patrício Aylwin has been welcoming the Communists and Socialists we managed to root out in 1973. Where does it get us that Pinochet is still commander-in-chief of the army? Pinochet is a shadow of what he once was. He's become a gaga old man, manipulated by his corrupt and obtuse family, his heirs clinging on to what little power they have left. While I, and others like me, who took a chaotic, poor nation out of the hands of incompetent people like Salvador Allende and transformed it into today's rich, dynamic Chile, find there's no place for us.

'But why did the advertising man move to a house in Jardim Paulistano all of a sudden?' he insisted.

Antonio ignored the question. He switched on the radio. A woman's raucous voice blared out, Madonna. She was singing a dance tune, accompanied by a backing group.

He changed stations. This time it was Phil Collins's crooning voice.

He changed again. Another female voice, Gloria Estefan, but this time almost childlike, with the same syrupy beat, singing in English again.

He spun the dial in search of a song in Brazilian, but could not find one. It was as if that evening all the radio stations in

São Paulo were broadcasting from somewhere in the United States.

The Chilean pulled up at a red light. He was disturbed at the news of the move. Eleven months' planning gone to waste. The Organization in Santiago wasn't going to like it. He knew the information was accurate. He'd trusted Antonio from the time they'd met during the period when they were hunting down Communists, in the months following the fall of Allende, when the Chilean military brought in specialists from Brazil and Uruguay to carry out interrogations. Antonio had had vast experience in the intelligence services in São Paulo, and he was the most successful. He had an incredibly persuasive way with informers. The Chilean had learned a lot from him. The only thing lacking was any sense of the pity that Antonio's wheelchair ought to arouse in him.

He analysed the new situation. When the advertising man lived in Alphaville, a recently built development outside the city, he was obliged always to leave and return by the same route, to and from a smart area of the centre of São Paulo. It had already been established where, when and how they were going to intercept his car, force him out and abduct him. His move to Jardim Paulistano complicated everything. There were countless roads and avenues connected to that neighbourhood. Nearly all the houses and mansions were surrounded by high walls. Many of them had armed guards. The Organization in Santiago needed to be told. Would the plans be postponed? Abandoned?

'The lights,' said Antonio, pointing to the green light now showing.

They drove down an avenue the Chilean did not recognize. He found everywhere in São Paulo hard to identify. Some parts were so dull and grey they reminded him of Berlin at the end of the sixties, when he had received his first training in interrogation techniques from US military assessors, together with five other agents from the Chilean intelligence services. He changed gear in silence. Antonio said nothing either, simply pointing right or left when they had to turn.

All those thousands of dollars gone to waste. The investors were not going to like that useless expenditure one bit. Eleven months pouring money down the drain. Four experts, based in Argentina, Paraguay and Peru, brought here since mid-April, in addition to Antonio and himself. The farm rented among sleepy towns in the interior where it would be safe to keep the advertising man for the time needed for the ransom to be paid. The flights between Santiago and São Paulo, São Paulo and Buenos Aires, Buenos Aires and Asunción, Asunción and Lima, Lima and Santiago, while the other four members of the team were being hired. More flights between Santiago and São Paulo, from São Paulo to New York, from New York to São Paulo. The days spent in Manhattan, in the luxury apartment rented at an exorbitant rate on 72nd Street, right opposite the advertising man's property, following him on his trips with the young blonde woman to the boutiques and restaurants on Madison Avenue, night after night of unbearable musicals on Broadway, afternoon visits to museums, cultural centres, and shop after shop run by Brazilians on 46th Street, until, finally, they had their reward: they saw him go all alone into the discreet building on

52nd Street, where on the spacious top two floors that were the New York base for the Israeli bank, both the Organization in Santiago and the advertising executive held accounts. Then the return to Paraguay to buy four small cars, plus this Monza, as well as a black Ford-100 pick-up, a Combi and a van with the lettering of an Osasco laundry, all of them with their chassis numbers erased, cloned licence plates and perfectly legal-looking documents. Counterfeit identity papers and passports, dollars to pay off the frontier guards, to rent the separate apartments on the outskirts of the city, for each member of the team, plus his in Guarulhos; bribes to waiters, valets, cleaners, porters, delivery men, gardeners, traffic police, office boys, florists, postmen, mechanics, child-minders, nightwatchmen, lift attendants, street-sweepers, shop assistants, newspaper boys, all the people who were given a dollar here, two dollars there, in the places the advertising man frequented or where he was in the habit of going, so many tips slipped into so many hands over the eleven months that he had lost count.

Antonio switched the radio off and said something he didn't hear properly.

'What did you say?' the Chilean asked.

'Armour-plated,' came the reply.

'Armour-plated what?'

'He's started going around in an armour-plated car. It's a Mercedes-Benz like the other one, but this one is silver. And he doesn't drive any more. He's employed a driver who is also a guard. His wife and son use the blue Mercedes now. The wife's driver is an ex-military cop. Both drivers are armed.

The house is guarded twenty-four hours a day. Two people, from a reliable company. And CCTV cameras everywhere.'

'Damn it, all these new factors upsetting our lengthy, painstaking plans: now this armour-plated car. With a guard. Armed. And probably well trained. Do you have any idea why there are all these changes?'

'Orders from Brasília.'

'Brasília? Why would that be?' The Chilean is genuinely surprised. Did Brasília order him to move? Did Brasília decide he should use an armour-plated car? Were the armed drivers also an order from Brasília? The house under surveillance the whole time, the—

'Everything. All the changes. All planned and carried out on direct instructions from Brasília.'

'So it wasn't the advertising man's decision.'

'No, it wasn't.'

'So Brasília has its own reasons for wanting him to be well protected,' the Chilean concluded. 'They're afraid he might be abducted. They know about us.'

'No. They're worried about his company. Leaks. Stolen documents. The revelation of bank account numbers in Switzerland, Belize, that kind of thing. The money that's been handed over to the advertising guy since the start of the political campaign last year.'

'Only to him?'

'Mainly to him,' said Antonio, quoting sources that he still knew and did business with in the now officially extinct but still operational National Information Service.

'If that's the case,' argued the Chilean, 'kidnapping the

advertising man would bring the whole world down on our heads. However furious the reaction from Brasília, even if they put the federal police on our tail, even if their associates lined up the best hitmen from Alagoas or Pernambuco to eliminate us, that would be nothing compared to all the search and rescue teams those banks and international financial institutions would set on us,' he explained. 'Once they calculate all the implications that abducting the advertising man could have, the Organization in Chile might even decide to hand us over. Not to mention the huge fortune involved. How much of the election campaign finance went undeclared? How much did they receive from all those interested in the privatization of state companies? How much more besides . . .'

In Miami I would be happy, thought Antonio as they crossed a desolate area close to Plaza Roosevelt. A beggar wrapped in a blanket went up to a group huddled round a bonfire and threw a small wooden box on the flames. Happiness is easy in Miami. And if not happiness, if not happy in the way of the silly dreams my brother Paulo has, then at least relieved not to be surrounded by whores and drug addicts like all these people here. I would forget my humiliating dismissal from the National Information Service by those corrupt arseholes in the new government after almost two decades of loyal service. Miami. Or Fort Lauderdale. Or Tampa. Miami. Miami is best. I don't mean a house on the same island where Emerson Fittipaldi has his mansion, but a high-class place. A Mustang 5.0 convertible in the garage. Or it could be a Camaro. There's another good area, what's it called, it's older. Coral Gables, that's it. The pavements in Miami all have ramps. Being in a wheelchair is not a constant problem. It's not a humiliation twenty-four hours a day. In Florida all the pavements have ramps. In every city I've been to in the United States, the pavements have ramps. The cinemas have special areas. I could even have my own store. Far from here. In Miami. Olavo's worth a good few hundred thousand dollars. I want some. I have a right to them. They'll soon be in my account. There is a way.

'We can't kidnap the advertising guy.'

'No, Antonio. We can't. It's impossible. I'll consult the Organization in Santiago to decide what to do next. Early tomorrow morning.'

'There's no need to consult anyone.'

'I'm sure there is. Today if possible, or early tomorrow.'

'No, there's no need. I've got the answer.'

'With an armour-plated car? With guards organized from Brasília? With—'

'We're not going to kidnap the advertising guy,' Antonio cut him off. 'We're going to kidnap somebody who is worth as much as he is. Or more. Somebody who is of no interest at all to Brasília, but who will force Olavo to give us all we ask for. We're going to kidnap his son.'

8

HOW LONG HAVE we been in this traffic jam? We left home at least half an hour ago. Longer still. What time is it?

'Is the school far off?'

'No, we're close now.'

'You said we'd be there in twenty minutes. We've been in the car more than half an hour.'

'It's the traffic, Dona Mara. I've no idea why it's so slow. Perhaps there was an accident. It's only a few blocks away.'

On the pavement outside, people were hurrying past. In São Paulo people were always in a hurry, she thought. A big fat woman was carrying several shopping bags. A thin man in a brown overcoat stumbled and bumped into her. A cabbage fell out of one of the bags and rolled into the road, where almost immediately it was crushed under a wheel. An old fellow was waiting to cross at the lights. Three young girls in school uniform were laughing at something one of them had said. The smallest of them was a redhead. Red-haired, dark, blonde, fat, thin, ugly, pretty, tall, small, old, young: these and a few other descriptions were enough for Mara. They were what peopled her world.

She turned her attention back to the car interior. The boy drawing. The Major sitting still. She didn't have a magazine to read, nothing to keep her occupied.

'Switch the radio on.'

The Major obeyed, reluctantly. He liked silence. The grating voice of a presenter rolling his 'r's flooded the car: *The minister considers that the withdrawal of eighty per cent of the money in circulation demonstrates the efficacy of the Collor Plan. Between March and June, inflation fell from eighty-one per cent to nine per cent. According to the minister . . .*

'Get rid of that. Find some music.'

He twirled the dial, skipped more news channels, and finally found a woman singing a slow ballad.

'Leave that. That's nice.'

It was from a film she had seen in New York, with Olavo. With that fair-haired actor who won the Oscar, and that black singer with the extraordinary voice, Whitney Houston.

She played the part of a singer in the film. He was her body-guard. At the end they were no longer together. Or perhaps they were, she wasn't sure. She didn't understand English that well. She understood a bit. Enough to speak a phrase or two in hotels or in a taxi, but not much more. She had never taken an English course. She had learned a little in her secondary school, and a little more in Porto Alegre, but that was all. Olavo spoke English. He spoke and read it very well. He studied it of course: his father the lawyer had insisted. English and French. In the department stores, museums, restaurants and bistros, it was always Olavo who spoke or read. Just as he did when it came to the contract for the purchase of the 72nd Street apartment.

She would love to understand the words of that song. She knew the meaning of *I will always love you* and a few other words. But that wasn't enough. She needed to know more English. With their frequent trips to New York, now that they had the apartment, now that she was the owner of a Manhattan apartment, there was no way she could carry on knowing so little. Perhaps she could do an intensive course. No. A course, in a classroom with a bunch of kids, she couldn't do that. She would have lessons with a private tutor. Olavo could find her one.

'We're there,' the Major informed her.

Apart from the plaque on the wall, the school was no different from the other dingy houses in this lower-middle-class neighbourhood which since the seventies had been gradually taken over by new residential properties. There was a bus stop almost opposite. A traffic warden was standing beside the school, a wad of parking tickets in his hand. The Major spotted him.

'I'll park on the next block.'

'No. We've taken too long as it is. Pull in here.'

'The warden . . .'

'Stop opposite him. I'll take the boy in.'

Mara took the sheets of paper and the pencils out of the boy's hand, stuffed them into the backpack, picked it and the boy up, opened the car door and got out.

The traffic warden closely studied the blonde woman

carrying the very blond, very pale boy in her arms to the school gate, which was opened by a teacher.

The boy went inside, and the teacher closed the gate. The blonde woman returned to the Mercedes-Benz. The car pulled away.

The traffic warden walked on two blocks, then got into a maroon Monza. Behind the wheel was an oval-faced man with curly hair.

Back inside the Mercedes-Benz, Mara was surprised at the silence.

'Did you switch the radio off?'

'I turned the volume down.'

'Turn it up.'

She did not give orders out of arrogance, even though she might consider herself entitled to do so in view of her elegant tailored suit, which cost the equivalent of four and a half months of the driver's wages, or the jewels gleaming on her ears, neck and wrist, which could pay several years' rent on the one-room flat in the run-down centre of São Paulo where he had been living since his divorce, or her handbag, which once belonged to the Princess of Monaco, but because in the world where she grew up, the urgency to want, need, get something did not permit the weakness (or the hypocrisy) of adding that word: please.

The Major did as he was told. He had dared turn the radio down because he thought his boss's wife would not notice or care. He obeyed her order as if he was unaware of the indiscretion of doing what he wanted in this luxury vehicle that did not belong to him. In his own life he had learned from an early age that those who gave the direct orders were not the ones who had the real power, but they did have access to the other, powerful people. Employees do not challenge their bosses, or express disagreement. That was unhelpful when it came to tips or favours. And he wanted to ask a favour, although he didn't yet know how to do so. Not for himself, but for Barbara. A rich woman like Mara must know people who could give his daughter a job. It could be in a shop. Barbara was not pretty, but if she were done up a bit, and wore decent clothes, she could work in one of the boutiques where Dona Mara was a customer. Barbara was well educated, responsible, she had good manners. She could also work as a childminder. She liked children. She could replace the childminder of one of Dona Mara's friends at the weekend. Anything would be better than emptying out rubbish and cleaning bathrooms.

The American woman singer with the powerful voice had come to the end of her declaration of eternal love. The presenter said her name, and added that the song was number one in the US hit parades. Then he announced a song whose title the Major did not understand, 'The Winner Takes It All'. After the first few bars he realized it was another love ballad, but this time sung by several singers.

Boring. Really boring music. He couldn't understand what they were singing, but he could understand the lament and self-pity. Weren't all songs the same? I'm unhappy, the person who loved me has left me, I can't live without him or her, and so on?

'Put some Brazilian music on.'

He spun the dial, until the needle reached the far end of the available stations, stopping at each one and then moving on. He finally found one playing an old song in Brazilian Portuguese, which he vaguely recognized.

> *Because those out of tune*
> *Also have a heart*
> *I photographed you with my Rolleiflex*
> *And it showed your enormous—*

The singer's nasal voice was interrupted. There was a roll of drums and the blare of trumpets:

> *We are interrupting our transmission to bring our dear listeners some news just in from Berlin. A short time ago in the former German capital, the authorities announced that the much-anticipated reunification of West and East Germany was to go ahead. And the date has already been set. This historic event, which will finally lay the Cold War to rest, will take place on 3 October. The split between the two Germanies occurred when . . .*

'Turn that off.'
'Yes, Dona Mara.'
'I want to listen to Brazilian music.'

All the radio stations were broadcasting news or foreign music, more foreign music, and more, until at last he found a male duo singing a folk tune with a rhythm like the ones his grandmother from Minas Gerais used to like.

There's a veil of tears over my eyes
Telling me that you're gone
And not to keep on weeping like this
I've done everything to convince myself,
To prove that life is better without you,
But my heart will not be fooled . . .

The Major left it on. Mara did not complain: she didn't seem to be listening. She had lit her cigarette and was taking a puff now and again, holding it between the fingers of her left hand.

I live inventing passions to escape my loss
But after the bed reality returns
And I feel your lack all the more.
There's a hole in my heart, a great hurt
My body wants your body inside it
I survive in a world without peace . . .

The gold lighter was still in her right hand, her handbag open. She was staring out of the window, but was not interested in what was going on outside.

She was thinking of the boy – so blond, so delicate, so light – whom she had just carried in her arms. How old could he be? He stroked her neck. As she was handing him over to the teacher she saw his arm reaching out and he raised his face close to hers, as if he was about to give her a kiss. She pushed him away just in time. She didn't want him to smudge her make-up.

69

Why did he try to kiss her? Why the hug? Let's hope Olavinho would never get it into his head to start that kind of public show of affection. She was horrified by that sort of scene: it was increasingly common in parks, squares, streets and shopping malls to see children and mothers hugging and kissing each other as if they hadn't seen one another for centuries. How ridiculous! None of that is necessary to show love for your child. My mother was never one to hug or kiss me, to caress me, none of that sort of thing. And yet she did love me. A lot. She still does. She did everything she could for me. When she still worked as a maid she altered all her bosses' daughter's clothes to fit me, she kept my school uniform impeccably clean, she would wash it at night and iron it so I could wear it the next day, she bought me the best shampoos, and although the make-up she bought wasn't always perfect, she did buy me lots; from the age of eight she took me to modelling auditions; when she got a job in a textile shop in the centre of Porto Alegre she went with me to every competition and beauty contest for Miss Porto Alegre Teen, Little Rose Princess, the Queen of This, the Miss of That; she was always by my side, buying fashion magazines and copying as best she could the styles worn by Hollywood and soap-opera actresses. It was a start. A good start. Not the best. But everyone has to start somewhere.

She never won a beauty contest, but she met people who found her modelling jobs, which she did in several cities in Rio Grande do Sul state, and occasionally in the capital, Porto Alegre. She appeared in adverts for well-known electrical goods stores there too, and then was auditioned for others in

São Paulo and Rio de Janeiro. Out of this came opportunities to have dinner with different clients, and . . .

A life that came to an end when she met Olavo, when they were choosing people to appear in a beer advert he was producing. She didn't get a part, but, well . . . well, that was where her new life began. Her happiness. Not in the way she had imagined, but . . . Happiness, yes, that was it. Because happiness is . . . To be happy you need . . . Happiness is having what she has, for example. Peace. Tranquillity. A beautiful house. The possibility of travelling abroad. Beautiful clothes. All the clothes she desires. All the shoes she desires. In Paris, Rome, Miami, New York, in Brazil itself. All she has to do is go into a shop, choose what she wants, and take it. No. Arrange for it to be sent. Or let the Major pick up all the bags and boxes while she saunters in front of him, mind elsewhere, strolling round the shopping mall under the eyes of all those who once looked down on her, when she was the girl-wearing-altered-clothes-from-the-daughter-of-her-mother's-employer. No longer. Never again.

Happiness is also having a son like Olavinho. Intelligent, cheerful, curious. Healthy. Completely different to her own brother. Vicente lived in bed. He hardly ever spoke. He was so thin. So pale. So different to Olavinho, who is tall, dark-skinned, energetic, always talking and asking why this, why that, talking, talking, asking questions, asking, talking, asking, running, asking, running, never stopping. A healthy boy. That's what healthy kids are like. Her brother Vicente scarcely got out of bed. She would go to school in the morning and come back late in the afternoon, almost at nightfall, and it

71

seemed as if he had not even moved beneath the bedclothes. He was very still. Very. His blue eyes (bluer than hers) followed all their mother's movements as she made soup, baked bread, prepared some oatmeal porridge. Vicente's bed was as close as possible to the stove, the warmest place. She remembered their tiny house, where the three of them slept in the same room, as always being cold. Until Vicente was taken away to the hospital. She can remember the streams of water running down the walls, especially in the icy July and August nights. But by then it was just her and her mother sleeping in the house.

Now Mara is going to pick Olavinho up from one of the most expensive schools in São Paulo. She is going to take him in one of the world's best cars to the most chic shopping mall in the wealthiest city of Brazil. They'll go to see a film, then do a bit of shopping, then they'll have a meal in a good restaurant, perhaps that one with French cooking on Nove de Julho, the La something or other, or the steakhouse on Haddock Lobo; yes, a steakhouse would be better. Kids love steak. Me too. I hope he doesn't start asking too many questions. He'll talk a lot. He'll be surprised that I've come to collect him from school. I'm no childminder. We have people who do that. He'll want to know why it's me today. Because I love you, I'll tell him. Just like that. Then we can talk of other things. What other things? He'll talk. Talk a lot. About lots of things. What he has learned in school and will want to teach me, what he said to the teacher, what he thought, what he didn't think, where he went to, what he ate in the snack bar, what his teacher is like, what his class is like, who his best little friend is, what that girl he detests is like, the one who hit him, or who he is always hitting, his maths exercise – no, he's not old enough yet to do any maths exercises. Or perhaps he does. I haven't seen his school books, I don't know what he studies. It's not necessary. It's a good school: more than that, it's the best. Olavinho already speaks English. He understands everything in English and can speak it. He reads English. Olavo wants him to go and study in England or Switzerland. Or in the States. I'm in favour of that. Totally in favour. The sooner Olavinho goes, the better he'll adapt to the new country and its customs. Now we have the apartment on 72nd Street, we can always go and visit him. And later on he'll be able to meet us in New York, spend the weekend with us, or something of the sort. He's going to be very curious about why I've come to collect him. He's going to ask lots of questions. He asks questions all the time. And talks all the time. In the cinema, the shops, in the car, in the restaurant . . .

The cigarette had gone out between her fingers. The long ash fell on to the carpet. She crushed the butt in the ashtray. Flicked the lighter on and off several times.

'Major,' she called out.

'Yes, Dona Mara?'

'Turn round.'

'Turn round?'

'Go back home.'

'Does madam no longer intend to pick up the—'

'Turn round.'

'Yes, Dona Mara.'

'After you've dropped me off, come back and pick up Olavinho and the housekeepers' boy.'

'Your son Olavinho gets out at two o'clock. The house-keepers' boy . . .' He said the name of the pale, blond child, but Mara did not hear him: '. . . is in school until three or half past.'

'Pick up Olavinho, drop him off at home, then come back and collect that deaf and dumb boy.'

'Yes, ma'am,' the Major acquiesced, signalling to turn left.

9

To LOVE IS a verb that only makes sense in advertising, thought Olavo as he leafed through the portfolios of titles and storyboards for the campaign approved by the state electricity company chairman.

For the love of your children you leave the place where you have lived your whole life without protest. To love is to allow your existence to change in the name of a future others are luring you with. To love is to cup air in your hands and think you have captured the key to life on earth . . .

To love must have been invented in order to sell something. Language had not been codified, but the verb To Love was already essential for the commercial survival of the nearest Neanderthal man. When the cave paintings of Altamira or Vale da Capivara are finally deciphered, the archaeologists will confirm that they say: You're Going to Love Our New Formula Clubs, or To Love is to Serve Bison Steak Without Additives. Thirty thousand years on, we paint on advertising hoardings or on TV screens: You're going to love the new Elion margarine. To love is to protect, washing your children with

Dubox toilet soap. I loved every mouthful of Clinton Nuggets. Happy and in love snuggled up in Pelobon quilts.

He paused at a photomontage of a wide expanse of vines weighed down with bunches of ripe grapes. In the distance could be seen the sluices of a giant hydro-electric dam. Probably a Canadian one. Or from the north of the United States. They were more photogenic. In the foreground, a hearty peasant smiled, with all his front, side and back teeth shining white. He was carrying a hoe over his shoulder. Behind him stood a tractor. He had not been aware before now that something was redundant. One or other item had to be got rid of when the final version of the photograph was produced. The hoe. It conveyed too much idea of effort, weariness and anachronism. The tractor was more modern, more efficient, more up-to-date. And he had to remind the art director that the model should have a thicker nose and darker skin, closer to the fantasy people had of a typical Brazilian. This was one of the adverts aimed at the foreign press.

He no longer went to the photoshoots. Nor to the filming of the adverts. Nor to the casting. He no longer had time for that kind of supervision. He was no longer the creative director-who-does-everything of the niche advertising agency, as he had been five years earlier when he entered a photographer's studio where they were choosing the model for a beer commercial and saw her for the first time. Among several other tall, long-haired blonde women lined up in their swimming costumes, smiling and as similar-looking as dolls on a shelf, second-rank models hoping for a good fee as extras. Not because she was the prettiest. Nor the one with the most voluptuous body. She didn't have the vacant look of good models, the face on which it's possible to paint any intention.

Even frozen in her professional smile, he could spot an awkwardness behind her chalky white face, beneath the excessive make-up. He didn't know if this came from her, or from his perception of that unknown young woman. On an impulse, he got his assistant to invite her to dinner, something he never did with the models. Even those with whom he ended up having some kind of relationship were never seen in public with him. He appreciated his twelve-year marriage to Selma, and wanted to shield their two daughters, Alice and Carolina, from any embarrassment. A dinner in an out-of-the-way restaurant would be an exception. From there they would go to a hotel. Period.

But the blonde stranger turned his invitation down. And his second one, made through the model agency. He discovered her name, plus the fact that she did not live in São Paulo, together with a telephone number in Porto Alegre. He left a message on her answering machine. Mara Elizabeth Grunnert did not return his call. He phoned twice more, left fresh messages; again with no response. He found out her address, sent her flowers. No reply. The next time, he sent flowers and a ring. Mara sent the ring back. He sent the ring a second time, with another bouquet of flowers. The ring was returned with a note of thanks, in looped handwriting leaning to the left. He arranged a meeting with a client in Porto Alegre at the end of an afternoon, and invited her for dinner. She arrived on time, only lightly made-up this time, her hair in a ponytail. She looked younger. She said she was grateful for his attention, but asked him not to try to contact her any more. She was engaged to an engineer from the Furnas electricity company. She showed him her engagement ring, and told him she was going to get married in two months and move to the interior of the state, taking her mother with her.

Olavo let her talk without lending any importance, or even listening, to what she was saying. Let your hair down, he said, interrupting her. She fell silent. Olavo insisted: let your hair down. And then at once, surprising even himself: come upstairs with me. I want to see you naked. She lowered her eyes. I want to see you naked, he repeated. I want to lick you all over. I want to . . .

Delicately folding her napkin on the plate, she raised her head, murmured Thank you, goodbye, then stood up and left the restaurant. It was only then that Olavo realized. What seemed like an imbalance in Mara's face was a vulnerability that dispelled the arrogance common in women who are self-confident about their own beauty. He was moved, and felt even more aroused.

He caught up with her in the street, just as she was getting into a taxi. He begged her: don't go. He begged her: stay with me. He begged her: forgive me. He begged her: have dinner with me, nothing more than that, have dinner with me.

Mara got out of the taxi. His marriage came to an end a few minutes later. In her long, thin arms, covered in the same golden fuzz (almost silvery depending on the light) that formed a thin trail down from her navel to her pink sex, which he licked as hungrily as he used to as an adolescent in the brothels of Belém, and where he liked to push his dark penis, leaning on his arms to keep their bodies separate and watch himself, furiously entering and pulling out of this light-skinned woman, until at last he came and collapsed on top of her, sweaty and satisfied, dimly aware that she could hardly breathe because she was almost crushed by the weight of his body, sometimes with tears in her eyes, which gave him even greater pleasure.

Mara was his, much more so than the house in Jardim Europa and the one on the beach at Maresias, than the cars he had dreamed of in his youth, the prizes at the advertising festivals in Venice and Cannes, his bank accounts in tax havens, the growing confidence the president of the republic's advisers had in his discretion. There wasn't much more he wanted. A pied-à-terre in Manhattan, for example. The apartment on 72nd Street belonged to the minister, as would the next one, in Central Park South, that he was going to sign the paperwork for in a few days' time. But the one after that would be his, just as soon as he could work out how to avoid the US tax authorities. On the Upper East Side. Preferably close to Park Avenue. Or on the avenue itself, around 80th Street, now that the New York property market was so weak. Then he would buy an apartment in Paris. On the Rive Gauche, which had so much more to offer creative people than the Rive Droite, full of stupid tourists and Arab potentates. Possibly in the Marais, in a quiet street like Rue de Jouy. Or on Rue Beautreillis, where he had rented a flat in the summer of 1985. It was a big place, but like an oven. All flats in Paris needed air-conditioning. On both banks of the Seine.

Hmm. He had to bear in mind that the president and the ministers were happier on the Rive Droite. And that this was where the boutiques were that their wives and lovers liked to go shopping in.

Ernesto came in without knocking. He was carrying a back-pack in his left hand. He was not alone. The big guy next to him was wearing a crumpled suit. His tie, made of synthetic material to look like silk, had a pattern that Olavo could only make out clearly when he came closer: birds that turned into fishes, then back into birds. Escher made in China, he imagined. An unlikely couple, he thought, shifting his attention from the Hermès tie to the backpack with its Walt Disney stickers that Ernesto had just put down on the marble floor, his handmade Church shoes, and from them to the cheap Vulcabras rubber-soled ones worn by his companion, whom he had just presented. Olavo only registered the last few words:

'A federal police inspector?'

Why were they here? What had brought them into his office at this time of day? Without warning?

'Did you say Inspector Vieira?'

'Vieri. Don't worry, he's one of ours.'

I'm not worrying, thought Olavo. I'm more annoyed at this intrusion. But I'm calm. Why shouldn't I be?

'Doctor Ernesto asked me to accompany him. To give support at a time like this.'

Support to whom? What for? Who was asking for support? This wasn't a moment for chatting. This was a moment when he needed to be left alone, in silence, with his own thoughts and calculations.

'Sit down, Olavo.'

'I'm fine here. I'm working. This is a really bad moment to interrupt me.'

'Sit down. It's better you do.'

He needed to study the media plan for the campaign. To make the final adjustments. We've already talked about the trip to New York. I've accepted the inevitable. I'll go. I'll sign the contract to purchase the minister's apartment. That can't be what Ernesto wants me to discuss with an inspector from the federal police.

'Sit down, please. And stay calm.'

'You can say what you have to say, Ernesto. I'm fine standing here. I need to finish what I was in the middle of. On your behalf. On our behalf. Our campaign. What do you need to tell me?'

It was not Ernesto who spoke, but the big inspector with the made-in-China Escher tie.

'Do you know Carlos Roberto da Costa?'

'No.'

'Yes you do, Olavo,' Ernesto interjected, taking a seat. The two other men remained standing. 'He's your wife's driver.'

'Ah, the Major.'

'A retired lieutenant from the military police,' the inspector clarified.

'Whatever you say. Why are we talking about him?'

'Did you know him well?'

'Of course not. He was one of our drivers.'

'We were the ones who hired him,' Ernesto explained. 'Him, the other driver, and the security guards for the house. Every

81

one of them recommended by our people in the National Information Service.'

'Retired lieutenant Carlos Roberto da Costa, aged thirty-six, was killed by five shots at the wheel of a blue Mercedes-Benz registered in your company's name. One shot to each shoulder, three at the back of the head. He was practically beheaded. There are several different-calibre bullet holes in the car's bodywork.'

My blue Mercedes-Benz, thought Olavo.

Our blue Mercedes-Benz, thought Ernesto.

'The bullet holes indicate that the gang attacked Lieutenant Costa from in front and from behind. We do not yet have any information as to how many of them there were. So far, there are no witnesses. It was a lightning operation.'

'My car is armour-plated.'

'Yours is, Olavo. But not this one.'

'But you said that . . .'

'What is important is that your car is armour-plated, Olavo.'

'This was no common attack, sir. Lieutenant Costa was executed. His weapon, a Glock 22, an incredibly efficient gun used by the North American police, was not even fired. It's an expensive weapon.'

'We supply the weapons for Doctor Olavo's bodyguards,' Ernesto explained.

'Lieutenant Costa did not fire a shot. It was a lightning operation.'

'You've already said that.'

'The good news is that there were no traces of blood

on the back seat. The boy can't have sustained any injuries.'

'The boy?'

'Sit down, Olavo.'

'What boy?'

'Sit down, Olavo.'

'They left this note.'

'What boy are you talking about?'

'It would be better if you sat down, Olavo.'

'They will probably contact you today, or at the latest tomorrow, to establish the ransom terms. We're going to need to intercept your calls here and at your home.'

'Phone-tapping? No way.'

'It's necessary, Olavo.'

'That's the procedure, Doctor Olavo.'

'I have confidential conversations with my clients. I carry out transactions that cannot come to light. I won't allow any of my telephones to be tapped.'

'With all due respect, Doctor Olavo, we don't need your permission. We're investigating a crime.'

He could feel himself breaking into a sweat. He hated sweating.

'Ernesto, you know we can't have anyone listening in to my calls. Remember the conversations with the Fat Guy? The money from the election campaign? The sensitive transfers? You know all that. Tell the inspector here that we can't have any phone-tapping.'

'We already are, Doctor Olavo. It's the procedure.'

His Pancaldi shirt was beginning to stick under his armpits. He walked over to the air-conditioning dial by the entrance, turned it to the lowest possible temperature, then came back to the others.

'This is an abuse. We're no longer in a dictatorship.'

'Sit down, Olavo, and stay calm. I've told the Fat Guy not to phone you until we've resolved this situation. He's in Zurich. From there he's going on to Lausanne.'

'I know. I speak with him almost every day. And I'm going to need to carry on speaking to him.'

'We'll use other people.'

'There are details about our dealings that only he and I know.'

'You can trust our group. Others will take care of the Fat Guy.'

Olavo wiped the sweat off his brow with his shirt sleeve. Other people in the loop meant more risk of leaks. And more sharing. The inspector continued with his explanation.

'First of all, they're going to call here or at your house. You'll have to choose a telephone there and another one here so that these people have a direct line to you. Those numbers must stay free. When they call, you are going to have to stay calm. Talk to them without haste. You have to give the impression of calm and that you agree at least partially to their demands. But you don't have all the money they are asking for. You need time to collect the amount they want. Doctor Ernesto here is going to use his links with the press to put a stop to any reports that could hinder our investigation.'

Olavo noticed the backpack at Ernesto's feet. The rubber material and the stickers. The trip to Orlando. Mara and him surrounded by the figures of Mickey and Minnie Mouse, Goofy, Donald Duck. Sandwiches that tasted of styrofoam, pails of watery soft drinks, queues, children shouting, shopping bags filled with baseball caps, T-shirts, pencils, figures, notebooks, trinkets, that backpack. That backpack. That backpack?

He sat down.

'The car was removed from the crime scene, Doctor Olavo. Your neighbours in Jardim Europa have no wish to publicize an armed attack outside their residences. Lieutenant Costa's body . . .'

'Are you telling me that . . .' He turned towards Ernesto. 'Are you and the inspector here to tell me that . . .'

'Lieutenant Costa's body is at the Forensic Institute. His family has not yet been informed. Doctor Ernesto thought it better to get the investigation under way before we located his relatives.'

That backpack. Had they bought it at Disneyworld?

'We do not know why Lieutenant Costa failed to react. We cannot directly accuse him of having been part of the attack. We have no proof that he was eliminated by his colleagues because for some reason they didn't trust him. We do not yet have any proof of that. Everything points in that direction, but we need to find the evidence. The investigation is only just beginning. We know that Lieutenant Costa grew up in a *favela* and has friends in those kinds of places.'

'Did you bring a friend of drug traffickers to work in my house, Ernesto?'

'Keep calm, Olavo. Our people are checking the

information with agents we can trust from the former intelligence services. Your driver may be innocent.'

'Innocent? A guard who doesn't react when he is being attacked by bandits?'

'We're still investigating that, Doctor Olavo. We'll soon have the necessary proof. The important thing now is to think of your son's well-being.'

'My son?'

The inspector pointed to the backpack.

'They left this behind. On purpose. To show they had him.'

'That backpack doesn't belong to my son.' He straightened up. 'That cheap backpack isn't my son's.'

Olavo rose from the table, went over to the telephone on the glass-topped steel writing desk, dialled a number.

'That cheap backpack isn't my son's,' he repeated while waiting for someone to answer. 'Hello, Irene? Yes, it's me. No, I don't want to talk to my wife. I want to talk to my son. Call him.'

He waited, a triumphant smile on his face.

'That cheap nylon backpack,' he said, pointing his chin towards it, 'is something you can buy in any store on Rua 25 de Março here in São Paulo. My son doesn't use crap like that. Hello, Olavinho. Hello, sonny. Daddy wanted to hear your voice. Daddy was missing you, that's why he called,' he said, casting a defiant glance in the direction of the big inspector with his made-in-China Escher tie. 'To hear your voice. Did you eat already? Did you eat already? Steak with fried potatoes that Irene made for you? What about dessert? Coconut pudding? Oh, yummy. And how was school today? Oh, how nice, you learned about life on a coffee farm in Africa? A coffee farm in Kenya? Good, good. Daddy is proud of you, son. Which driver picked you up at the English School? Which one? Oh, it was the Major. What time did the Major collect you? You don't remember? But it was the Major who fetched you from the English School, wasn't it? After lunch? OK, Olavinho, Daddy loves you. When he gets home, Daddy will come into your room to give you a kiss. Now call Irene, because Daddy wants to talk to her. A kiss to you too, sonny . . . Irene? What time did the Major pick up my son from the English School? He dropped Olavinho off at home at three in the afternoon? Where did he go after that? To pick up your son? Why? Who gave instructions for the Major to get your son from the deaf and dumb school? Ah, Dona Mara said he could. No, Irene, I've no idea where they are now. Held up in traffic, probably. Don't worry. Don't say anything to Dona Mara. Is there any ice cream in the house? Give Olavinho some.'

10

THE TWO SMALL cars left the state highway, one close behind the other. Headlights dipped, they travelled along the poorly asphalted local road that was slippery from the light rain that was falling. Almost four kilometres, until they reached a wooden gate with barbed wire that was opened by a nimble, broad-shouldered youth in a woolly hat. A Magnum .357 was concealed under his dark parka jacket. All the details of the operation begun three hours earlier were going exactly according to plan.

The Ford F-100 was the first vehicle they had changed, leaving it only a few blocks from where they had carried out the abduction, its doors unlocked, the key in the ignition and all the documents that had been carefully counterfeited and brought in from Paraguay left in the glove compartment. They transferred the trunk in which they had put the boy to a smaller, white pick-up with the fake picture and address of a laundry in Osasco on its sides. This was swapped for a tinted-windows Combi at a service station on the road out of São Paulo, then later for a grey Fiat Uno with a Minas Gerais number plate in the already dark parking lot of a chain of roast chicken restaurants. When they left there, it was accompanied by a maroon Chevrolet Kadett hatchback, with a plate from Valença in Rio de Janeiro state that was fake like all the previous ones. Less than two hours later, the two vehicles reached the exit marked Piedade–Ibiúna–Pilar do Sul–Votorantim. That was where they turned off.

During the journey, they spoke only when essential. They talked to each other in Spanish. Their accents were South American, but with different rhythms and expressions.

After closing the gate, the man in the parka and woolly hat got into the second car. The two vehicles climbed the hill, bumping over the gravel track until they reached the bare brick house with a sloping roof that was a crude imitation of an Alpine chalet. There were cheap pine shutters on the windows, the middles cut out in heart shapes, as the builder imagined was done in the Austrian Tyrol. The only light came from a lamp close to the veranda. Like many other properties in the region, the house had no electric light, which was why it had been chosen. There were no neighbours in the vicinity. The man on guard outside, rifle in hand, was stamping his feet on the ground in a vain attempt to keep out the cold.

The cars parked side by side, their lights still on. One of the passengers from the Kadett went into the house and lit another lamp. The driver of the Fiat and the man in the parka opened the boot, took the trunk out, and carried it easily into the house. The other passenger in the Kadett, the man with an oval face and curly hair, followed them in. The thin, older man who had lit the lamp lifted the lid of the trunk. He pulled out the sack and carried it in his arms. Pushing a chair out of the way with his feet, he placed it on the table, undid the rope, and began to open it.

The first thing they saw was the boy's startlingly blond hair. His pale face. Closed eyes. His unmoving head.

They pulled away the sack. The boy did not move.

Their first reaction was one of surprise and hesitation. The man with indigenous features stepped forward to look at the child more closely, then moved back. 'What's wrong with him?' he asked, worried.

'Either he's asleep or he died of suffocation,' said the Peruvian, who had come in from keeping guard to see the result of the kidnapping and to get some relief from the cold, even if only temporarily.

They turned to look at the man with the curly hair and oval face, waiting for a reply and instructions. He went up to the table, pressed his first and middle fingers against the boy's neck, and felt his pulse.

'He was shut in the trunk for too long,' he said.

'Is he still breathing?' the youth in the parka wanted to know.

'Yes, he just won't wake up.'

'He's wet himself,' said the older man, pointing to the boy's soaking shorts. 'Take his clothes off, and put him in some dry ones.'

They glanced at each other. Nobody moved.

'There aren't any clothes for him,' the Bolivian said eventually.

'Why not?' the older man wanted to know.

'Daniel didn't tell us we should buy any,' said the Bolivian, trying to justify himself.

'We don't use people's names in here,' the curly-haired man reprimanded him, raising his voice.

'No, of course not. Sorry.'

'Nobody told me to buy pyjamas or any other clothes for him,' the Bolivian repeated.

'Nobody?' asked Emiliano, the older man.

'Nobody asked me.'

'Nor me.'

'Me neither. None of us knew we were supposed to buy clothes for the kid.'

'It doesn't matter. You, the Uruguayan,' said the curly-haired man pointing at Emiliano, 'you stay with him tonight. Tomorrow morning it's your turn,' he said to the youth in the parka, 'you tomorrow afternoon' (pointing to the Bolivian), 'and then the Uruguayan again tomorrow night. You, the Peruvian, can sleep in the daytime. I'll take turns on guard with you.'

'What about food? When do we feed him?' asked Emiliano, coming back in carrying a yellow acrylic blanket.

'Three times a day, no more. In the morning, the afternoon, and at night.'

'What if he gets hungry? Hungry kids cry a lot,' said Emiliano, taking off the boy's shoes, shorts and underpants.

'If he cries, slap him.'

'His socks are wet too. He peed a lot. He must have been very scared. Better throw the socks away as well. Alfonso . . .' He corrected himself. 'You, give me a pair of your socks,' he said to the guy in the parka and hat. 'The nice thick ones. I know you've got some.'

'They're too big for the boy.'

'Give me them, damn it. What does it matter if they're big,' said Emiliano angrily. 'The kid's cold. Can't you see that?'

The boy was covered in goose pimples. His teeth began to chatter.

'Just bring them, damn it. Go on. Get the socks. You've got a woollen pair. Bring them, Alfon— bring them, for God's sake.'

The younger man tore off his woolly hat, threw it on the floor, turned on his heel and stormed out to his room.

'Don't provoke Alfonso, *viejito*. You've done other operations with him, you know he's a bit crazy.'

'He can keep his craziness. This kid is worth his weight in gold, isn't he?'

'He's worth hundreds of thousands of dollars for each of us. You're right, *viejito*. The kid has to be in good health. At least until his father meets our demands.'

The shaven-headed youth brought in the socks, rolled up in a ball. He threw them to Emiliano, who caught them, unrolled them and began to put them on the boy's feet.

'The kid's hot. He's got a fever. Bring me a thermometer,' he ordered, to no one in particular.

'Is there one? Where?' asked the Bolivian, following a few moments' hesitation.

'I don't know. In some drawer or other. Go and look.'

The man with ruddy cheeks opened the drawers in the

house they had rented two months earlier, then looked in the bathroom cabinet, and in the kitchen.

'Hurry up.'

'There are no thermometers here. I can't find any.'

'Bring me something to get his temperature down.'

'What sort of pills?'

'What does it matter, damn it. Any you can find. Whatever there is. The boy's burning up. His fever's getting worse.'

'There's only a half-full bottle of fruit salts. A bar of cocoa butter. Iodine. Cotton wool. Plasters. That's all.'

'No analgesics? Not even aspirin?'

'No, there's nothing else.'

'So send one of them into town, Daniel,' he said to the man with curly hair.

'We don't use names in here, *viejito*.'

'Go fuck yourself, Daniel. This kid has a high fever. Look how he's curled up shivering. Tell one of the others to go to a pharmacy in town.'

'Are you feeling sorry for him, *viejito*?'

'He's our investment, Daniel. We need this boy. You brought me to Brazil to deal with a wealthy adult. Instead of that, you got me to kidnap his son. That wasn't what we agreed. Not me or any of us. I don't like it. None of us likes it. But you left us with no other way out. So what have we got here and now? A sick child. Feverish. Tell one of them to go and get something for his fever. And get them to bring a thermometer as well.'

'If you want, I'll go,' said the indigenous-looking man with the ruddy cheeks. 'I know where the pharmacies in Pilar do Sul are. I can be there and back in thirty minutes.'

Daniel nodded in agreement.

'Go with him, Argie,' he told the shaven-headed youth. 'Take the Fiat. And bring me two packs of cigarettes.'

The two of them left. Emiliano carried the boy to the bedroom, where the only window was barred with vertical wooden slats. Daniel followed him.

'I don't like you talking to me that way,' he said, closing the door behind him. 'I'm in command. That was what the Organization in Santiago decided. You have to respect the decisions I take.'

'Like hell I have to follow your orders,' said Emiliano, laying the boy on the bed. He picked up a woollen coat, and threw it on to the bed against the wall. He kept the 9mm Walther in his waistband. He was never without it.

'Don't you think the others agree with me, Daniel? That they too find it absurd to carry out this kind of operation with a kid? We're professionals, Daniel. How often have we worked together? In Venezuela, Chile, Argentina, Peru, Colombia: how often? But never with a kid, Daniel. You never told us our target was a kid.'

'It wasn't, Emiliano. The situation changed. Here's why . . .'

'Our plan was to leave the adman beside some highway in Paraguay, after the ransom was paid. I've already advanced part of the money to the frontier police in Ciudad del Este and in Foz do Iguaçu. On both sides of the border, the police were expecting us to go through with an adult, not with a boy of what . . . three, four or five?'

94

'It makes no difference to them. What they want are the dollars.'

'You want us to leave here, cross the whole state, then into Paraná and across that too, and then enter Paraguay with this kid in the boot? Alive?'

Daniel did not respond.

'This is an idea of that Brazilian colleague of yours, isn't it, Daniel? Kidnapping a child is that cripple's idea, isn't it?'

'Antonio isn't a cripple. He was left paralysed in an operation against subversives in the Brazilian jungle. And we don't use that word "kidnapping". This is an operation for the transfer of funds.'

'Go fuck yourself, Daniel. And go shit in your sister's cunt while you're at it.'

'When four hundred thousand dollars are deposited in a Caribbean bank in your name, Emiliano, you won't regret it. And you won't even remember the colour of that boy's eyes.'

They fell silent. They had nothing more to say or accuse each other of.

'Fuck. Fuck, fuck, fuck, fuck,' said Emiliano under his breath.

'Tomorrow,' said Daniel, 'before we change the guard on the boy, and when he's got over this fever, I want you to record the first cassette we'll send to his father. Get him to say: "Papa, if you love me, pay for my life." Get him to say: "I don't want to die, Papa.' Or: "I'm scared of dying, Papa." Something like that. If you think he needs to be crying a bit, slap him. Hard. Record the message when you hit him, so that the father can hear. Record him crying. Get the boy to say: "They're beating me, Papa. Don't let them beat me, Papa."'

He slammed the door loudly. Eyes tight shut, the little blond boy showed no reaction.

11

IT WAS PAST nine o'clock by the time she finished emptying the last rubbish bins. She was hungry and late. She wanted to arrive home in time to re-read her classroom notes, do the exercises, and still be able to get some rest before Tuesday morning, when she would arrive at her course later than usual. She had to help her mother get the furniture and equipment out of the hairdressing salon from which she had been evicted for failing to pay the rent. She would see the few customers she still had in their own homes and apartments.

She took off the green linen jacket with the name tag that identified her as Barbara, General Service Assistant. She hung it on the plastic hanger in the locker they were given inside the staff toilet. She pulled the grey-and-blue-striped acrylic sweater on over her cream blouse, put on her navy-blue nylon coat, picked up her backpack and slung it over her narrow shoulder.

She was all alone in the lift as it took her down seven floors. Although she was hungry, she didn't open her backpack to take out the wholemeal bread sandwich with sesame paste she had brought from home. She didn't feel comfortable eating in public. She didn't like people seeing her chew, and did not like seeing others eating. Unlike other young people her age, she avoided going into pizzerias or snack bars. Not just to save money or because she did not eat red meat. To see jaws moving, lips twisting to right and left, forks plunging into mouths, teeth sinking into bread: all these facial contortions made her feel queasy. She always found a way to have her meals at different times to her mother and stepfather. She should have eaten the sandwich in the staff toilet. It would have eased her hunger until she reached Barra Funda. But she hated the toilet and its permanent smell of excrement and disinfectant.

She went out into Rua Maria Paula. A light rain was falling. She hurried towards the metro station, protecting herself from the drops under the few awnings along the way. Turning the corner, she went down Rua Santo Amaro. Someone called her name. Or a name similar to hers. The street was deserted. She heard her name again. She turned to look back. It was a young man. Thin and lanky. He also had a rucksack. She didn't know him.

'You walk quickly,' he said, out of breath.

'Who are you?'

'I was waiting for you.'

'Why? Who are you? How do you know my name?'

'It was written on your name tag.'

Barbara blushed. She was embarrassed to be identified as a General Service Assistant. Embarrassed that somebody had noticed her in spite of her green uniform: she thought she became invisible once she put it on. Just as until now the people who scrubbed floors, cleaned windows or scoured sinks had been invisible to her. She did not know how to respond to this new situation. She turned her heel on the young man and started walking off quickly once more.

'Wait! Barbara!'

He ran to catch her up.

'Wait. I want to talk to you. Wait!'

She kept on going, feeling the raindrops beat against her face. The boy followed, and caught up with her.

'My name is Luís Cláudio. I'm studying English too. Forgive me for coming up to you like this in the middle of the street. I didn't dare talk to you in school.'

'Why?' she asked, coming to a halt and confronting him. 'Were you ashamed to talk to a cleaner?'

'No! No.'

'Are you trying to pick me up?'

'I've already seen you loads of times. I'm in the class immediately after yours.'

'Leave me alone,' she said, setting off again.

He followed, staying a short distance from her. By now they were in Avenida Vinte e Tres de Maio, getting close to the metro station.

'You're going to Barra Funda.'

Barbara did not reply.

'I know.'

They reached Anhangabaú station. Both of them were soaking wet.

'I've followed you before.'

99

Barbara halted. She said, trying not to sound frightened:

'Did you also know my father lives near here? In that building over there: can you see where the light is on?' She was making all this up. 'That's my father's apartment. He's with the police, the military police. I'll go and call him, I will.'

The boy lowered his eyes. He tried to smile, but did not succeed.

'I'm sorry, so sorry, Barbara. I followed you because you leave school late. I've followed you more than once. It's dangerous to use the metro so late at night. I wanted to be sure you got home without a problem. That's why I followed you. I'm sorry, Barbara. And since it's raining today, I thought I could try to talk to you . . . and to . . .'

He unzipped his rucksack and took out a folding umbrella.

'I always bring one. Would you like to use it?'

Barbara laughed.

'You have a nice laugh.'

Barbara blushed again. She hated it when that happened, and hoped he hadn't noticed.

'Can I accompany you home? My name is Luís Cláudio.'

'I know, you already told me that.'

On the way to Barbara's stop, he told her he was from the interior of São Paulo state, the north-western part. He said he was the youngest of four children, two boys and two girls. Livia and Laura were married, in the Promissão district of the city. They had children of their own, and were housewives. His brother Leonardo had emigrated to the United States, via Canada. He worked in the construction industry with other Brazilians, in a city whose name he couldn't remember, but which was close to Boston. Leonardo was trying to get his Green Card, but hadn't yet saved enough to pay an American woman to marry him. Once he got the card, he would take Luís Cláudio to live there. That was why he was studying English. For now, he was living in a rented room in the centre of São Paulo, which meant he could walk to class. He paid for it by doing computer work. Sometimes he also did deliveries. That was why he knew nearly all the names of the metro stations. And he knew the routes of dozens of buses.

'Name somewhere in the city, and I'll tell you how to get there.'

Barbara laughed a second time.

'I like it when you laugh. I've never seen you do it before. You don't laugh very much.'

Again, she did not know how to respond.

'Do you want me to tell you something funny?'

Barbara nodded.

'Do you know what my surname is?'

She waited.

'Grosso. My full name is Luís Cláudio Grosso, "Fatty" Luís.'

They both laughed. The train reached her station. They went out into the street. It was still raining. Luís Cláudio opened the umbrella. Huddling together beneath it brought them close to each other. They said nothing for a few minutes, both of them ill at ease. Barbara was the one who broke the silence.

'Me too, sometimes.'

'You too, what?'

'I also think about leaving.'

'To emigrate?'

'Yes.'

'To go to the United States?'

'Yes. Or to Portugal. I know people who have gone there. Several of them. A neighbour of ours is leaving soon. She's got a tourist visa.'

'It's better in the United States. There's more work. It's harder to get it, but it's worth it. They appreciate people who work hard there. You have got thirty years to pay for a house. The prices don't change. It will cost the same tomorrow as it does today. People plan what they are going to do in a year or even five years' time, things like that. My brother wrote me that he doesn't want to return to Brazil. If he gets his Green Card, he'll only come back to visit.'

'I can't go. My mother has money problems, my father is retired, my stepfather has to pay maintenance to his ex-wife and son. I can't go. They need me. But I think I'd like to. If I could, I think I'd like to go.'

All of a sudden she desperately wanted Luís Cláudio to ask if she would like to emigrate with him, but instantly felt ashamed of what she was thinking. The idea also came into the boy's mind that he should say to her: it would be good if we went to the United States together. But neither of them allowed their wishes to surface and be spoken.

'Barbara, what job would you like to do?'

'Bilingual secretary. If I knew English, I could get a job. A lot of foreign firms are coming to Brazil now. With what a bilingual secretary earns I could help my mother and still be able to study. I want to take the university entrance exam.'

'What in?'

'I'm not sure. And you?'

'I'm not going to try for university. I'm going to the United States. As soon as Leonardo sends the word, I'm off.'

They reached the two-storey building where she lived. The rain had eased off. They said goodbye without arranging to meet again, without even exchanging telephone numbers, although they both knew they would see each other again. Barbara went in. She climbed the stairs to the apartment at the back where she had moved four years earlier, when her mother opened the beauty parlour in the next street. She found her mother seated at the dining table. All the lights were on. The apartment had been ransacked. Her mother almost leapt out of her chair.

'The police were here,' she said, her voice strained and loud. Realizing this, she tried to tone it down: 'The federal police.'

Barbara looked at the mess in the room.

'They searched everything.'

'What for?'

'They took your stepfather with them. They think he could be an accomplice.'

'Henrique? Whose accomplice?'

'Your father's. They found IOUs in Henrique's name in your father's flat. Together with our address.'

'IOUs?'

'Your father's been helping Henrique. Lending him money.'

'What money? My father doesn't have any money.'

'From his retirement pay-off. I always thought it was

money from when he retired from the military police that he was lending Henrique. For us.'

'My father doesn't have any money to lend. He doesn't even have a telephone.'

'It wasn't his retirement money. It was from drugs.'

'Ma, have you gone crazy?'

'Your father has links to drug traffickers. The federal police found out. They found drugs in his flat. Your father's in jail. Incommunicado.'

'Where?'

'They didn't say. Nor where they were taking your step-father. We have to find a lawyer, Barbara. We need to do something. I've no idea where to start. I don't know any lawyers. Do you?'

Barbara didn't know if she did or not. She didn't recall ever having met one. At that moment all she could remember was what she'd seen when her father opened the door to his tiny, filthy flat on Rua Riachuelo. She remembered every stick of furniture. There was so little of it. A pizza box. A stove with two burners. An empty refrigerator. Her father had mentioned a job as a driver. And security guard. Perhaps he had said a name. She couldn't recall. She wasn't certain whether her father had mentioned somebody's name. But there must be some clue to it in his flat. Some indication. To get in she would need a key. She didn't have one. But the care-taker must surely have a copy. They always did in that kind of building. If he didn't, they could break in. Or possibly he knew the name of her father's employer. Or the address where he worked. Or . . .

She ran out of the door. Her mother shouted after her, but Barbara went on running until she reached the metro. She got on in the direction of Anhangabaú. It was only when she was halfway there that she remembered the thin cigarette paper her father had given her the week before. She rummaged in her backpack until finally she found it. There was a phone number on it. The last digit was blurred.

12

SHE HEARD THE commotion on the ground floor, louder than usual at that time of night. She heard other voices as well as Olavo's. His usually loud voice was occasionally replaced by what she thought were the sounds of other men. Two or three different voices; she was not sure. Nor was she interested in finding out. Perhaps Olavo had guests for dinner. He had probably agreed the menu with Irene. He always dealt directly with her. That did not bother Mara. She did not know (and had no interest in learning) how to combine hors d'oeuvres, main course, soup, salad, fish, poultry, sorbets to refresh the palate between this and that, dessert, coffee, liqueur. Besides which, she had spent the afternoon in bed with a migraine, and had left instructions that she would not take any phone calls.

The three or four men must be having drinks. Whisky, certainly. Olavo had probably offered them some wine. He liked to demonstrate what a connoisseur he was of vintages and types of grape. Or perhaps he had kept the wines back for their meal.

She realized she couldn't hear any laughter. They must be discussing some serious matter. They were probably talking about things to do with Brasília. About people from the capital, no doubt. When she was near they avoided talking about positions or surnames. They only used first names: Fernando, Marcílio, Bernardo, Zélia, Leonel, Pedro, Teresa. She couldn't give a damn whether they did this in order not to reveal anything, or to demonstrate what close friends they were with the powerful. She hadn't the slightest interest in those people, or in that kind of conversation. When their wives were with them, it was even more boring. They talked about their houses, fashion, interior design, children, employees, gossip about people in Brasília she didn't know.

She had to get up. Put some clothes on. Do her hair. Then her make-up. Wear some high-heeled shoes so that she was a head taller than the guests, as Olavo liked. A pair of earrings. A necklace. A bracelet. Open the bedroom door. Walk down the corridor. Down the stairs. Cross the hall, enter the living room. Smile. Greet each of them. Say something to each of them. Accept whatever drink Olavo offered her. Invite them all to transfer to the dining room, and withdraw if it was a business dinner. If not, she would have to wait for Olavo to seat every guest at the table. Sit down, so that the men could sit down. Smile. Make conversation. Eat. She wasn't at all hungry. She had less and less appetite. But she would go down and play her role as soon as the butler knocked at the door to tell her that dinner was almost ready. But first, she had to get up.

She got up.

Now I have to choose what to wear.

She walked barefoot across the soft, thick vanilla carpet. The bedroom was nice and warm: the central heating worked perfectly. She could wear something light, even though it was cold outside. She opened the wardrobe. She hesitated at the sight of the row of dresses, suits, blouses, trousers, most of them gifts from Olavo, or bought on his recommendation. She chose a greenish blouse and a brown skirt. She tried them on, then changed the blouse for a cream one with small splodges that looked like blue flowers but were in fact hazy squiggles. From the rack opposite she chose a maroon pair from among the dozens of shoes, and put them on.

She went back to the bed. Sat down on it. The exclusively male conversation was continuing down below. She could hear a word every so often, but no complete sentences.

She stretched out. Closed her eyes.

Dozed off.

She woke up when she felt something pressing on her chest. She opened her eyes. Olavo was sitting beside her. He was pressing and moving his hands over her breasts. It was painful. She groaned. He smiled. She wanted him to stop, but didn't know how to make him do so.

'Somebody attempted to kidnap our son,' he said, slipping one hand under her blouse until he was touching her left breast.

Mara tried to sit up. He pushed her back on the bed.

'This afternoon. Close to here.'

The hand under her brassiere began to caress her nipple.

'They attacked your car.'

'My . . .'

108

'Your Mercedes-Benz,' he said, pulling and tugging at the nipple. 'Lots of shooting.'

Mara groaned. Olavo slipped his other hand inside the blouse, pushed up her brassiere and grasped her right breast.

'They killed your driver. They executed him. Three shots to the back of the head.'

'The Major . . . ?'

'His head was all but chopped off.'

He was still twisting her nipples with his fingers, more and more roughly.

'A gang. Drug traffickers. The Major was one of them. They stopped the Mercedes-Benz in a street near here. He pretended they were being ambushed. He didn't fire a shot.'

Mara bit her lips. She wanted to resist the pain. Wanted to stop groaning.

'He . . . ow . . . the Major was . . . he was brought here by . . . ow . . . your friends from Brasília.'

'He came recommended. So were all the new staff. By people from the former intelligence service. They're investigating. It must be an organized gang.'

Olavo let go of one of her nipples, cupped her left breast in his open hand and squeezed it. He went on twisting the right nipple. Undid the buttons on her blouse. Pushed the brassiere up above the breasts. Round, heavy, pale against the dark skin of his hands. He squeezed even harder. Mara groaned again. He dropped a hand to her thighs, groping at her through her skirt.

'There are two patrol cars outside, with plainclothes policemen. I brought in four more guards for inside the house. I sacked the previous ones.'

He pushed his hand up her skirt, as far as her knickers. He could feel the pubic hairs round her sex. He began stroking her.

'Nothing will come out in the news. The Major's body is on the slab at the Forensic Institute as an unidentified corpse. No one is going to gain access to it until all this has been resolved. Officially he is in jail, incommunicado.'

He pulled her pants halfway down her thighs. He caressed the soft down surrounding her vagina. He gave her a little smack, a dry slapping sound. Another smack, then a third, a fourth, a fifth: sharp, rapid taps, the sound of skin on skin.

'They left a piece of paper saying: We Have Your Son.'

'But you said that Olavinho . . .'

'He's fine. He's somewhere safe.'

'In his room?'

'They wrote two numbers on the paper.'

Olavo pushed the length of his finger inside Mara. She was dry and it hurt.

'Ow, Olavo. Please . . .'

'Two numbers. They're not ordinary drug traffickers.'

He twisted the finger inside her. Turned it round and round.

'Olavo, you're . . .'

'They're no ordinary kidnappers.'

He removed his finger, spat on it, pushed it back inside Mara, who shuddered.

'They haven't rung yet. The inspector says that it's deliberate. To leave me uncertain. Not sure whether my son is alive or dead.'

'But you said . . . Ow . . . Olavo.'

He undid his flies with his other hand.

'Get hold of me,' he ordered, taking Mara's hand and placing it on his swollen penis. 'Take it in your hand. Go on.'

'Olavo, your guests are down below . . .'

'Get hold of it. That's it. Now squeeze. Two numbers, Mara. Do you know what one of them is? Grip my dick, Mara. Harder. They know what the number is. All the digits. Ah, Mara, that's good. Harder.'

His big hand covered Mara's, forcing her to move it up and down. At the same time, his finger sliding in and out of her vagina.

'Quicker, Mara, quicker. Go on, yes. That's right. Go on. The digits. They know them. They're no ordinary crooks, Mara. Ah. Ah. That's it. Harder. Quicker. The numbers in the account. In my account. Go on, go on, go on. The New York account. Ah, ah. That's it. That's it. The account in the Israeli bank. Ah. My biggest account. The biggest. That's right. That's it. Go on. Like that. Ah, ah, ah, ah. Aaah. Aaah. Aaah. Aaah.'

He came on Mara's hand, in continuous spurts. A few drops fell on to the carpet and on the tip of one of her shoes.

Olavo relaxed, collapsing on to the quilt and across Mara's legs. His finger was still inside her.

Mara wiped her hand on the eiderdown. She parted her lips, thinking there must be something to say, about the two of them, or the attack that she didn't really understand, or the news that someone had been killed, a kidnapping, a note that was not exactly a note, two numbers on a piece of paper, or about her son, her driver, what else? But say what? Why? What for?

She struggled to push her body higher up the bed. Olavo's finger slipped out.

'Two numbers, Mara. They're no ordinary criminals. I don't know what to do. I don't know where this is going to end. Everything I've built up could come crashing down from one moment to the next. All because of a stupid driver. Linked to somebody in Brasília. Who? Who? Is it a group? If so, which group? Linked to whom? Defeated politicians? Businessmen who didn't win any contracts?'

Mara couldn't be less interested. At that moment all she wanted to do was get out from under his body. To go to the bathroom. Wash herself.

'Not even you know that number, Mara. I've never talked to you about that account. But they know it. They wrote all the digits. And they left another account number. Where they wanted the money transferred to. They know. They've had access. The money isn't mine. The account is in my name, but I'm simply representing other people who can't move abroad as freely as I can. How could the kidnappers have found out about that account? It must be people close to me, do you see? That's the money they want. They know it's not mine, but that it's in my name, do you see? That I have to transfer the money from that account to their account if I want to save my son's life, do you see? Our son's life, do you see?'

'No, Olavo, I don't see. You said it was a kidnapping. But that Olavinho . . .'

'Is somewhere safe. He doesn't even know what happened.'

'Have you put guards in his room?'

'He's not in his room.'

'Where . . . ?'

'By now,' he said, consulting his Cartier Santos timepiece, 'he's in a Lear jet on his way to Switzerland. He's headed for a boarding school there. We'll go and visit him as soon as this kidnapping has been resolved. The people who used to be with the intelligence service are investigating. Everything is going to be very discreet. Nobody wants this to turn into a scandal. Possibly the president's enemies. Maybe not even them. Because if there were a scandal, no money would find its way into anybody's account. My biggest fear is that this story could get out, into the press.'

'If Olavinho is safe, who then . . . ?'

'The housekeepers' son. That deaf and dumb boy. He was in the Mercedes. They must have thought he was our son.'

He wiped his hand on her skirt, getting rid of the last traces of semen. He stood up. He felt reinvigorated. Ready for the fight. It was at moments like this that his best ideas occurred to him. And now one had. To continue with the farce and take it further. To publicize the blackmail threat disguised as a kidnapping. To talk openly about the attack on the car and the boy's disappearance. To confront them. Go in the opposite direction to the one he had been taking. That was it; that was it! Long live the power of information and all it could do. The more that was kept hidden, the more power he was handing to his enemies, whoever they might be. And the more that came out, the less chance there was that he would have to transfer the money to them. It was not in the interest of the blackmailers, whoever they might be, to have the existence of secret accounts revealed. He would talk about the ransom money, saying they had asked for it in cash. In non-sequential banknotes. Nothing, absolutely nothing about the transfer of funds from one foreign account to another. He would present it to the media as an ordinary kidnapping.

He would start with television. He had influential friends in the country's major networks. Executives, partners, directors, owners who earned good money from the adverts placed by his agency's clients. All that was needed was for Ernesto to call one of them. It would have to be Ernesto, because he, Olavo Bettencourt, the creative, award-winning, charismatic owner of one of the biggest advertising agencies in Brazil, was in no fit state to do so at that moment of grief, no, not grief, grief only if the boy were dead. At the moment of anguish. Perfect: moment of anguish. At that moment of anguish it would be for Ernesto to inform them about the kidnapping, ask for their support to show the millions of television spectators who at that time of day would be watching another soap opera, to show them at first hand, in a special programme, the loving, dramatic, moving appeal of a suffering father and mother: please, please, don't hurt my little boy. No, not my little boy. Bursting into tears: don't hurt my son. Our son. It would be better to say his name. Make it more personal. This is not just any child, not just another disappeared youngster in the hands of heartless criminals. This is Olavinho. Our Olavinho. Please, don't hurt our Olavinho. An appeal with photos. That photo by the bedside. Father, mother and son. Together, the loving family. Mara looks lovely in the photo, the light lending her hair a golden halo. Ernesto could give details of the attack, on the soundtrack, as a friend of the family. After that, one of our media specialists can continue the work, putting out press releases, getting in touch with radio stations and newspapers, choosing the reporters I will talk to. A woman reporter would be better. Especially if she had children. There would be a natural empathy with my and Mara's suffering. Mmm. Careful with Mara. She won't know how to play her part properly. The way she speaks doesn't help. The grammatical mistakes she makes, those expressions from the south of Brazil she can't get rid of.

Keep Mara out of it. She should only appear by my side. In dark glasses. Her hair done up in a bun. There must be a dark-coloured suit in that wardrobe of hers. A fitted suit, not too high-heeled shoes, standing slightly behind me, hands crossed in front of her body. Quiet. Oh, and with a small hanky in her hands. Crumpled. As though she had been crying. While this is going on, Ernesto and people from the intelligence services take care of those bastards who want to get their hands on our money. On my money. And after all that, Olavinho appears, safe and sound. We'll bring him back from Switzerland. We'll get together to give an interview. We'll say the ransom was paid in cash, handed over in some lonely spot in São Paulo state. We'll supply all the moving details. I'll be the one who handed over the money. A fearless gesture. Fatherly love that knows no bounds. The criminals wore masks. They handed over my son, then disappeared down the highway. Ernesto can arrange all that. Even a photo with a telephoto lens, wobbly and out of focus, of the moment when I hand over a briefcase, possibly two briefcases, or a suitcase, with the ransom money. In the meantime, the federal police will have found the real kidnappers. They will have prepared an ambush: none of them should come out alive, or the plan will fall apart. They will all die. The solution is easy: the bandits died in a shoot-out with the police. That's it. All of them. However many there might be. They resisted capture, there was a shoot-out, yes, that'll do. The body of Mara's driver is presented together with the bodies of the other criminals. An ex-military police-man who has brought shame on the profession. Perfect. Perfect.

'Change your clothes,' he said to the woman stretched out with her eyes closed. 'We're going downstairs. We have to organize things with Ernesto.'

13

THE CROWD MOVED apart to make way for the man in the wheelchair. Anybody who didn't see him because they were staring at the platform in the distance, straining their ears to hear the words mangled by the dozens of loudspeakers, was warned by the person next to them or behind them. Everyone was concerned for him: some of them even touched him on the shoulder, or offered their hands in greeting even though he ignored them, feeling a sudden affinity because even a citizen with obvious problems in getting around had wanted to be present there, at that moment. Yet another Brazilian who was saying enough was enough.

Above him, in front of him, all round him, hanging from windowsills, tied to lampposts, strung across the iron railings in front of shops, stuck to walls and doorways, carried by groups and individuals, in twos and threes, bands of youngsters, rows of men in suit and ties, he saw painted cloth or plastic banners, pamphlets, placards, cardboard signs written in ink, flyers, Brazilian flags, red flags with the hammer and sickle on them, red flags with white stars. The streets leading to the square in front of the neo-gothic-style church were packed. And more people were arriving all the time, oblivious to the drizzle.

He reached a point where it became impossible for him to advance any further. One of the wheels of his chair got stuck on a grass bank, tipping it to one side. He was surrounded. He pulled back until he was completely on the grass.

There must be more than twenty thousand people here, he calculated. A lot more. Probably thirty thousand.

He looked around him again.

More than thirty. More than forty thousand. Sé square measured about fifty thousand square metres. Every corner of it was filled. So were the nearby streets and avenues, and the Dona Paulina viaduct. When our agents' photographs are developed I'll have a clearer idea, he thought. But there are more than forty-five thousand people in the crowd, no doubt about that. Or fifty thousand.

The big platform at the far end was built sufficiently high to be seen from all angles. Several dozen people were squeezed on to it. Politicians, trade unionists, performers. Several, many, were wearing yellow T-shirts. A presenter went through their names, gave instructions, called one or other of them out to give a speech or a rallying cry. He recognized him by the voice, which he usually heard in sports broadcasts: Osmar Santos.

Sometimes waving, talking together like old friends, he saw people whose files in his department of the National Information Service had grown and grown since the 1960s.

Ulysses Guimarães, Mário Covas, Leonel Brizola, Franco Montoro, Fernando Henrique Cardoso, Luiz Inácio da Silva, Chico Buarque, Henfil, Fernanda Montenegro – the same subversives from before, and some more recent ones.

My brother must be here, he thought. If Paulo has returned from exile, he must be here among this lot. Together with this sort of people. But he's still in Sweden. If Paulo had come back, I would have been informed.

Every speech was applauded, some with more enthusiasm than others. Like the one made by the union leader Luiz Inácio da Silva. At a certain point there was loud clapping as a procession went by carrying a black coffin, on which Antonio read the words *Indirect Elections* written in white.

The governor of São Paulo came to the microphone.

I've been asked if there are three hundred or four hundred thousand people here, shouted Franco Montoro, waving his left hand in the air. *But the answer is a different one. Here today we can see the hopes of a hundred and thirty million Brazilians.*

His words were greeted with an ovation. Some of the crowd began chanting a slogan that was taken up by thousands of voices:

> *One, two, three,*
> *Four, five, millions,*
> *We want our president*
> *Elected by all Brazilians.*

They've lost their fear, thought Antonio. Following the amnesty, the return of the terrorists who were abroad, after the end of secret detentions and interrogations in the military torture centres, after the end of control of the media and the removal of our censors from the newsrooms, they're sticking their heads up out of the slime. The rats are emerging from the sewers.

The first notes of the national anthem could be heard over the loudspeakers. Many in the crowd raised their right hands to their chests. Some of them had tears in their eyes. Almost everyone started to sing.

> *The placid shores of Ipiranga heard*
> *the resounding cry of a heroic people*
> *and in shining rays, the sun of liberty*
> *shone in our homeland's skies at this very moment.*
>
> *If the assurance of this equality*
> *we achieved by our mighty arms,*
> *in thy bosom, O freedom,*
> *our bodies shall defy death itself!*
>
> *O beloved,*
> *idolized homeland,*
> *Hail, hail!*

Poor homeland, he thought. Handed on a plate to people like this by an inept president unable to prevent the international crisis destroying our plan for a Great Brazil. A mediocre cavalry officer, anointed by that German Geisel, who could never choose between accepting the inevitability of repression in order to build the First World Brazil begun in 1964 and the disorder of a hypothetical freedom on behalf of an even more hypothetical democracy. We're going to end up in the hands of these corrupt nonentities, these Communists and Socialists we drove out of power twenty years ago. Two decades thrown in the bin. In times gone by, we could have put a bomb in the middle of this crowd. Or provoke some brawl that would publicly undermine the meeting. We've got plainclothes agents here in Sé square and even up on the platform, but what use are they? They're all forbidden to do anything. We've become puppets. We've colluded in this. Worse than that. We've become accomplices.

He spun the wheelchair round, his back to the platform. The people in front made room for him.

On the corner of Rua Rangel Pestana he passed four policemen in fatigues. There were lots of them in different areas of the square. Useless, every single one of them, Antonio concluded, hurrying away.

Eight floors above him, a tall, thin man wearing a coat despite being in his own office was closely observing what was going on in Sé square. At the same time he was unconsciously stroking his lilac-coloured tie printed with tiny red and blue dolphins, the almost perfect and much cheaper made-in-Taiwan imitation of an Hermès tie he had seen in a Paris duty-free shop. The sound reaching him, muffled by the double-glazing and the noise of the old air-conditioning his partner insisted on keeping on at minimum, was not clear enough for him to hear the words of the speeches made on the platform, which he had watched being built over the previous few days. But the banners were perfectly legible. Down with the Military Regime. I Want to Vote for President. The People United Will Never Be Defeated. Our Time Has Come. General Strike Against Hunger and For Direct Elections. I Prefer the Smell of Horses to the Smell of Figueiredo.

'You should come over here,' he said to the portly, dark-skinned man sprawled over sketches, layouts, proofs and photographs for an advertising campaign for a chain of supermarkets. 'You have to see this.'

'Don't disturb me. I have to get all the details right for these adverts. I'm going to have to spend the night here so that I can present the campaign properly tomorrow morning.'

'Don't get so worked up about it. It's my wife who's going to approve the campaign. It's more important for you to see what's going on down there, in Sé square.'

'I want this to be the best retail campaign in the history of Brazilian advertising. It will be. In the future, twenty, thirty years from now, they'll still be copying the ideas I've come up with in this work.'

'The future's right here, outside your window. And you refuse to leave your chair to come and see it. To see this demonstration that's so . . . so . . .'

He was searching for the exact word to describe the impression the dense crowd made on him. Olavo was busy comparing two almost identical photos. Both of them showed a married couple of around thirty sitting at a breakfast table. On it was a jug of orange juice, a coffeepot and another of milk, four cups, a sugar bowl, sweet and savoury breads, butter, ham, turkey breast, two kinds of cheese and a dish of curd cheese, two sorts of jam, a board with slices of melon and a fruit bowl with grapes, pears and apples. In the second photo, the couple had a six-year-old boy with them and an eight-year-old girl. The children were eating bowls of corn-flakes. In both photos, the plate in front of the father contained scrambled eggs and two rashers of bacon. The mother's had half a papaya on it.

'What's wrong in these photos?' he asked, interrupting Ernesto. 'Look closely. Look carefully. Here. Take them, take a good look. These adverts will be published here in São Paulo, in Rio, in Fortaleza, Recife, Salvador, in Belo Horizonte, Brasília, Curitiba and Porto Alegre. What's wrong in these photos? What's wrong in both of them?'

'Too much food?' said Ernesto after a few moments' thought. 'European fruit? Bacon and eggs boost cholesterol? Cornflakes are American children's food?'

Olavo took the photos back, and placed them side by side on the desk.

'The models. They're too dark-skinned. The consumers will be offended. In the south of Brazil because they'll see it as a black family. In the north and north-east, as a poor family. Black and poor are synonymous in Rio, Paraná, Minas, Ceará, in the whole of Brazil. Light-skinned, blond models are what give a positive image. I'll present them tomorrow as they are now, but I'll get the photos redone for the final version.'

Ernesto's attention had turned back to the demonstration. It was only two years since the Turk Paulo Maluf had been named as candidate and had won. That was the first time the military authorities had allowed a direct election for state governor. In November of the previous year, much to everyone's surprise, more than ten thousand people had congregated outside a football stadium in São Paulo to demand direct elections for the president as well. Before that there had been smaller demonstrations in state capitals like Goiania and Curitiba that did not seem to have much political impact. President João Figueiredo's response had been as crude as his personality. He increased censorship and declared that the protests were subversive.

'Now even he admits he's in favour of direct elections,' said Ernesto,' but drew no reaction from Olavo.

He did the calculation again. More than a hundred thousand people are in the square. Perhaps two hundred thousand. The panorama suddenly revealed offered him the kind of certainty he had felt when his future father-in-law had presented his daughter Adélia to him.

'We're going to be rich.'

This time his partner was interested. He put his pen down, swivelled the chair and waited.

'We're going to create the political campaigns for the candidates in direct elections. Including the presidential candidates.'

'Brazil's next president will be Mário Andreazza. He's already been chosen by the military. Without direct elections.'

'Possibly. But after him it will have to be a civilian. And he will need to campaign on the radio, the TV, in the newspapers.'

Ernesto understood that opportunities like this only came once in a generation. He was fascinated by the red and green-and-yellow flags being waved in the square below. All those people would discover a common goal. Even if it took ten years, and no more than that, possibly even only five, if this movement grew at the rate it was doing, the military would yield. It was the best way for them to be able to place their investments and their heirs in the industries and stable positions. They would allow the president to be chosen in direct elections. Just as they had agreed to direct elections for state governors. There would be candidates. Genuine ones and chancers. The candidates would have to run campaigns. Electoral campaigns involve huge sums. Millions of dollars. The entrepreneurs contribute, so do the cattle ranchers. Industrialists contribute, the oil multinationals contribute, so do the cigarette multinationals: money pours in from all sides. Part of it goes officially to the campaigns. Another part stays outside. Associates like him and Olavo could take that money to safe havens outside Brazil. Charging a reasonable rate for their services, obviously.

'We're fine with the Turk. He was a friend of my father-in-law's. He used funds from his bank accounts – those of my wife and in-laws – to show his thanks to the ARENA delegates in 1978. It was a favour he never forgot. Olavo, your first foreign bank account came after the Turk was elected, do you remember? Out of the money for the campaigns our agency created for organs of the state government. Was it in the Cayman Islands or in New York?'

It was a purely rhetorical question, and Olavo did not bother to respond. Ernesto went on:

'The Turk gave us connections to the old ARENA party. We won propaganda funds for two parties in north-eastern states. But the right is in decline, Olavo. The future is with the left. You only need to look out there.'

'The Turk's going to end up in jail.'

'"He steals but does things." Remember what they say? The people like him. As long as he's constructing tunnels and viaducts, and having bandits killed, they'll carry on electing him.'

Olavo went back to correcting the adverts. Ernesto turned his back on him. He was still amazed at what he could see in the square, streets and avenues down below him.

'There must be a hundred thousand people at the demonstration. Or more. We need contacts with the left, Olavo. Your wife is our way in.'

'Selma isn't a militant any more.'

'What do you mean? She collected signatures to help found the Workers' Party, she knows all the parliamentary deputies and senators of the PMDB, she helped organize protests following Vladimir Herzog's death, she took messages to the exiles in Paris, she was arrested when she was a student leader . . .'

'That was in Belém, in the early seventies. She has stayed friends with those people, that's all. Nowadays Selma devotes herself to our two daughters. She doesn't want to go to the theatre, the cinema, or anything that will take her away from them. She's a full-time mother.'

'Hasn't she just done some work for Fernando Henrique Cardoso?'

'That was more than a year ago.'

'What about that consultancy she did . . .'

'You and Selma can't bear each other, Ernesto. Your wife loathes Selma. And the feeling is mutual.'

Feelings weren't the point. What he needed were Selma's contacts. She could present them to the left-wing leaders, including the senator and two federal deputies for whom she had already acted as media adviser. Sooner or later the left would be sharing the funds with right-wing politicians.

'Give Selma a call. Invite her to dinner. Go to La Tambouille, or some other posh place. Show how proud you are to be sitting alongside her. I'll show up after dessert. Without Adélia. I'll find a way to introduce the matter.'

'I can't.'

'Of course you can. I'll tell Adélia we'll present the campaign the day after tomorrow.'

'I can't.'

'Go on, pick up the phone. Don't worry about those adverts.'

'I can't.'

'Then I will. I'll explain you're caught up in the supermarket campaign, and that's why I'm phoning. I'll say you've realized there could be some future opportunities, but that they're too complicated to talk about on the phone, and that you, or rather we, need to have a talk with her. Urgently. Tonight. A talk on which her daughters' future depends.' As he said this, he walked over to the phone.

Olavo got up to halt him.

'I can't. Not because of the campaign.'

Ernesto had already dialled the first numbers.

'Don't do that. Put the phone down.'

The receiver was still in Ernesto's left hand, but he stopped dialling.

'I can't. I have to meet someone tonight.'

'So what?'

Olavo took the telephone from Ernesto and replaced it on the cradle.

'I'm in love. Madly in love.'

Before Ernesto could start asking questions that might lead him to reveal more than he wanted to or should, Olavo told him he had met a woman.

He changed the length of time they had known each other from two months to ten. He changed the studio where he first saw her auditioning for the part of an extra in a beer commercial for a flight between São Paulo and Porto Alegre. He said, in a tone mixing pride and concern:

'She's fifteen years younger than me.'

'Fantastic. Go for it. Love is a wonderful thing, etc. But meet her some other night. Our dinner with Selma is more important.'

'I can't. Mara is all on her own in São Paulo.'

'Meet her tomorrow.'

'She's going back to Porto Alegre tomorrow. She lives there. She's engaged. To an engineer. She's going to marry him in a month. Or two. She was going to. The date was set.'

'Tell her tonight is impossible. That you've got a business meeting you can't postpone. Cancel the meeting with that woman, Olavo.'

'I can't. Tonight . . .' He opened his leather executive briefcase with the gold clasp where he kept his confidential documents, and pulled out four different-sized and shaped keys. '. . . I'm going to give her the keys to the apartment I bought on Avenue Casa Branca. So that she understands she can cancel the wedding to her Furnas engineer.'

'Have you gone mad? An apartment for your lover in the same neighbourhood where you live with your family?'

'She's not my lover. I'm going to separate. I'm going to live with Mara. I'm crazy about her.'

He was about to confide: Mara is the best fuck I've ever had. But he preferred to say:

'Mara is the love of my life. I want her to marry me.'

'No way! Not now, Olavo. This is not the moment to separate from Selma. It would be disastrous for our plans.'

'For your plans. Mine include Mara.'

'Our plans. Our future millions of dollars. Where did this woman who's driving you crazy come from?'

'Porto Alegre.'

'Who is she?'

Olavo kept his description to the basics: Mara is blonde, tall, beautiful, with chalky-blue eyes. He added: she was travelling with her mother. Then some more: she represented Rio Grande do Sul at an international tourism convention in Bahia. Again: she was Miss Porto Alegre. And again: Mara is shy, light-skinned and blushes whenever I pay her a compliment. Still more: Mara is an only daughter. And also: her mother is of Italian descent, her father is of German and Azorean stock. He added: her family owns a chain of jeweller's stores in the interior of Rio Grande do Sul. And again: her father died when she was a child. Again: Mara did not accept any of the expensive presents I tried to give her. More: Mara won't take any of my money, even to pay the taxi. He added: in her I've rediscovered all I lost with Selma.

'I'm crazy about her,' he repeated.

'Have you fucked?'

'No.'

'You haven't fucked?'

'Yes.'

'Yes or no?'

'I seduced Mara. She didn't want to. She's engaged. She didn't want to betray her engineer. I insisted. I did everything, tried everything to get her to go to bed with me. She resisted as hard as she could. But she finally surrendered. I gave her pleasure like she had never known before. She cried, Ernesto. She sobbed her heart out.'

'A good fuck is no reason to marry someone, Olavo.'

'Mara is much more than a good fuck. She likes being in my arms. She likes listening to me. Everything that Selma and I no longer say to each other, I say to Mara. We spend hours talking. She looks at me and I feel like opening up, being myself, showing myself the way I am. The way I used to be. The way I want to be. Do you know what it's like for a man of my age to find a woman who can do that to you?'

'Olavo, listen: that situation . . .'

'She falls asleep in my arms, Ernesto.'

'The crises in any marriage . . .'

'She's not interested in the girls' school, the girls' clothes, the books the girls are reading, the excursion the girls are going on, the braces on the girls' teeth; do you see, Ernesto? Selma is a good woman, a woman with lots of good qualities, an educated woman, it's just that . . . it was different when we were young. I'm still ambitious. She has become . . . Selma today is . . . She doesn't even listen to music any more. The sort she used to like: Coltrane, Bill Evans, Tom Jobím, Elis Regina: none of them. Her only interest is the girls. Mara's interest is me. Me. Me, Ernesto. I talk to Mara about my plans. My dreams. She doesn't think it's silly for me to want to be the top advertising man in Brazil. She admires that. She's proud to be with me. She wants to know about my past. I tell her what I was like when I was a boy in Belém. The books I used to read. The films I saw. The music I listened to. I say things that Selma thinks are boring, but that Mara finds really interesting. I help Mara discover worlds that her generation know nothing about. I talk about Jules Verne, Alfred Hitchcock and Grace Kelly. Cary Grant, Cyl Farney, Oscarito. Humphrey Bogart. Ingrid Bergman. Celly Campello. Rita Pavone. Nat King Cole. Ella Fitzgerald. Cole Porter. Jacques Brel, Nouvelle Vague, Jeanne Moreau, *Jules et Jim*, Jean Seberg, Belmondo, Jerry Lewis, Jacques Tati, Gustav Klimt, Brancusi, Modigliani. I talk about football, advertising, design, the Brazilian Jews who left Recife and went to found New York, the first Japanese immigrants who came to plant pepper in Pará, the Paris Commune,

131

the treasure of the Romanoffs, Cartier-Bresson's photographs, the way Venice is slowly sinking, everything. I talk about everything. Everything I no longer talk about with Selma. Mara adores listening to me.'

'But we need Selma.'

'I can't let Mara get married. I can't lose that woman.'

'I'm not talking about passion. I'm talking about millions of dollars. Stay married to Selma. Buy an apartment for this girl from the south . . .'

'Mara.'

'Buy Mara an apartment in another part of São Paulo. I'll look after everything for you. But don't separate from Selma now. Not yet. Travel with Mara. I'll create a smokescreen for you with Selma. Has Mara been to Paris? Take her to Paris. All women love Paris. No, not Paris. It's full of Brazilians. Go to New York. The dollar is expensive and prices are high, so you won't find any Brazilians in New York. I know of a sophisti-cated, discreet hotel on Park Avenue. Put your separation from Selma off for a year. Just a year. In that time we can organize dinners for people on the left. We'll become their friends. We'll connect them to those who can finance their campaigns. Just a year, Olavo. A year. Then you and Mara can live happily ever after. Now, come over to the window. Get up. Come here. Come and see the future I'm talking about. Come on.'

Olavo couldn't remember ever seeing Ernesto so carried away. So much so that he smiled at him openly, forgetting the embarrassment of his yellow buck teeth, usually hidden behind a tight-lipped smile.

'Come over here, Olavo. Come on.'

For a minute, perhaps two, Olavo still did not move. Then he pressed both hands on the edge of the desk and pushed the chair back. He stood there for a few seconds, slapped his thighs, straightened up and went over to the window. He folded his arms, but said nothing. The crowd in Sé square was slowly dispersing.

In half an hour it was empty. The few demonstrators who were still there or in the adjacent streets, some of them still carrying placards and flags, were trying to find the groups they had come with, or were saying goodbye to each other, embracing one another and then heading for the bus stops and metro station, wondering whether it mightn't be better to wait a while until they were less crowded so that they could travel home more comfortably. Public transport that day was free, courtesy of the state government.

Once relative silence had returned to the centre of São Paulo, the military police carried out their last order of the day. They marched in formation from Rua Rangel Pestana, where they had been on duty, towards the mini-buses waiting in Rua Federico Alvarenga to take them back to their barracks.

Sergeant Carlos Roberto da Costa walked towards the back seat, where he sat down. He wasn't the least bit interested in his colleagues' comments, and lit a cigarette.

The conversations were between policemen of similar rank. The two lieutenants in command of the group were surprised at the lack of trouble at such a big demonstration – no drunkards, no trouble-makers, no brawls, not even the usual pickpockets. There wasn't even any confrontation with the unionists and their allies. Further forward in the bus, a corporal and a sergeant were talking about the soap-opera actors and singers they had spotted up on the platform. None of them meant anything to him. Another corporal complained about the rain and his soaking uniform. Next to him the discussion was about how unfair it was that the Brazilian Zico had lost the title of player of the year to that Frenchman Michel Platini, and the selection of Sócrates and Roberto Dinamite for the Brazilian national team, which one of the talkers was against, and the other for.

Why did we come here? Sergeant Costa asked himself. To keep order? Was it a demonstration against or in favour of the government? There were people in the government giving speeches, and people opposed to the government also speaking. By now Barbara ought to be asleep. Her birthday party would be over, her mother must have put her to bed, and lain down herself. She will have left a plate with a piece of birthday cake and some sweets for me on top of the sink. If there were any left over. I don't mind.

He took a last drag on the cigarette, dropped the butt on the floor and crushed it under his boot.

What difference is voting for president going to make to people's lives? All politicians are the same. Is the president going to make things less expensive? Is he going to bring down the price of rice or bread or beans? Or meat? Or rent? No, of course he isn't. How can a president bring the rents down? He can't do anything. Ever since I was a boy, prices have risen and risen. And I know that in these last months everything has become dearer than ever. Just for Barbara's birthday it cost . . . I've lost count. And Kátia didn't do anything special. I saw some kibbeh, some cod croquettes, chicken balls – not much at all. It is for Barbara's little friends and some relatives: Kátia has probably also invited the two girls who work in the hairdressing salon with her, and one or two neighbours.

Everyone in the neighbourhood rents. One of these days I'm going to buy us a house. One day I'm going to get free of paying rent.

It could be a small house, then later on we can move to a larger one, when things improve, as I win promotions here and there, it doesn't even have to be a house, it could be an apartment.

We're going to celebrate my daughter's fifteenth birthday in a house of our own.

I don't like sweet things. But I wanted to be at my daughter's birthday. She would have liked me to be there. I wanted to. I would have liked to have sung her happy tenth birthday. I'd have liked to have a piece of birthday cake that Kátia made for my daughter. Our daughter. The cake she made to celebrate our daughter's tenth birthday. I'd like to have eaten a sweet she gave me. That Barbara gave me. I saw a plate of chocolate truffles, another of cupcakes, another plate of I don't know what. I don't really like sweet things. But I'd eat some of it if she gave it to me. Yes, I would. I would happily eat it.

I never imagined that one day I would have a daughter and that she would be ten and would have her own party, that I would be able to pay for. Me, who never had a birthday party in my life. She might think I didn't go because I didn't want to, but I did. Yes, I wanted to. But in fact I was relieved that I had to work this Wednesday. I prefer to. I love my daughter, more than anyone else: not that I love very many people, but I love her more than all the others. But it's better that I'm working today. There'll be lots of people there, and I'm not one to talk to many people. Or even to a few. However many there were at Barbara's party. I don't know. I'm not good at that sort of thing.

Why did so many people get together in Sé square? Just to show they want direct presidential elections?

Guaraná. I was Barbara's age when my aunt gave me my first guaraná drink. It came in a small bottle that must have been made especially for children. I loved it! Oh, how I loved it! How awful it was not to be able to have more than one. Not that Sunday. It seemed as though an endless number of Sundays would have to go by before I could drink another of those small bottles of guaraná. And so I never wanted to drink another one. I learned it's not good to want something you can't have. I remember that lesson even today. For everything. I only want what I know I can have. I only want what I can want.

I know I'm not very intelligent. But I know how to do lots of things and I'm a hard worker. I don't miss not having studied. I'd like to know more, I'd like to understand things better, I'd like to be able to reply to the questions I ask myself, but I'm not stupid. I have a good career in the police. I'm healthy. I am quick, I have good eyesight, good marksmanship, good instincts. I know the best thing to do in raids, I know if I should go down an alleyway, I know the moment to break down a door or to stand next to it and talk to the armed delinquent inside. I know. I never had to learn any of it. I see, I hear, I know.

At home, I don't know. I don't get it. Kátia talks, I try to understand what she says about me, or what she says about other people, I try to understand why she isn't satisfied, why she says she isn't satisfied, why she isn't happy, that she isn't happy, why isn't she happy? Why not? Is it so complicated for a woman to be happy? She can't say I'm not good for her, because I know I am. It's just that I don't like talking. I don't like chatting much. I'm not one to chat a lot. I don't want simply to listen. I know how to do things. I don't know how to talk. I never have. Whatever I want to do, I do it. But not talking. No. That doesn't mean I don't care. I do care. I like things. But I don't know how to say that I like things, that I care. When I speak, what I say is not what I think. What I think is better than what I say. So there's no point me speaking. I don't say what I would like to say. I say only what I can manage to say.

I do everything I can for her and Barbara. Everything. As much as I can. I buy what she asks for. Everything. I set her up in her hairdressing salon, I had to borrow money, I'm still drowning in debt from that, but that didn't resolve anything, for her it didn't resolve anything . . . She says it's not that, it's not about money, and I say that I can't manage to say what she wants to hear from me. I'm not like that. I wasn't brought up that way. She says I'm not there, and that's the problem. That I'm not at home enough. She wants me to talk and to be at home more. That's what she says is wrong. How can I be at home more? I have to work, I have to get on, do more shifts, do night-time security work, do whatever I can because I have debts to pay and because I'm not one to sit around at home. That's not how I was brought up. She has everything she wants. So does Barbara. I don't allow my daughter to want for anything. I never have. I never will.

Some day in the future, a few years from now, when she is old enough to sit for university entrance, I'm going to be able to pay for her studies. Barbara is going to be the first person in our family, in my family and in Kátia's too, who has a university degree. Whatever she wants. I'll guarantee it for her. I'll guarantee her future. I will. I will.

14

THE DELAY DID not seem normal to her. But because she was not yet accustomed to the problems caused by the traffic in the big city, Irene simply waited, without saying anything to anyone. She tried not to think about it, not to worry. She spent her time spooning the wine sauce over the roast beef in the oven, and preparing the marinade for the filet mignon, in case Doctor Olavo preferred to eat steak rather than roast meat. She washed vegetables for the salad, sliced the almonds to put with the rice if he decided to have the roast, peeled the potatoes she was going to cook in boiling water before she browned them in butter with grated onion – they could go with either the steak or the roast. She kept busy, but could not stay calm. When it was gone six o'clock, she went to find Stephan.

Her husband was putting away the stepladder and tools he had used to repair the laundry roof. She helped him pick up the bucket and hammer, and asked if he was hungry and wanted to eat soon. He said he was, but that first he wanted to have a hot bath. She didn't say a word to Stephan about how late the car was in which the Major was driving their son home. She didn't know how to. Stephan was against using their boss's car. And he had been against bringing the boy to the city in the first place. He thought the boy was slow-witted, and would only complicate their lives in São Paulo. He would be better off surrounded by sheep and the tobacco and strawberry plantations. Brought up by his uncle and aunt together with other children and relatives who understood him and did not laugh at him. He would learn to weed, to sow, to water plants, to harvest them. It was a good place for a deaf-and-dumb child to be. But Irene insisted. She thought that in the city the boy would at least learn to read and write. If they never returned to the farm in Anápolis – and she was hopeful that one day they would go back there, facing the green hills and looking out on the river that ran through the bottom of the valley – their son would be protected, living with his mother and father. Whatever happened. Alongside them. As he ought to be. He wasn't to blame for having been born the way he was, thought Irene as she made her way back to the kitchen. I'm the one to blame.

She heated the macaroni and vegetable soup that Stephan liked on cold nights like this, while at the same time she warmed up on a low heat the pans with rice, beans, pumpkin and rolled beef stuffed with carrots that was to be served to the staff of the house. She set the table, added paper napkins, and was about to take the pans off the stove when the security guards came into the kitchen. They were accompanied by two uniformed policemen. Irene was sure something must have gone wrong. Very wrong.

Guillermo the Bolivian took another turn round the small town. He went up and down the empty, dark streets of Pilar do Sul a second time. The cold rain made the asphalt greasy.

He could not see an open pharmacy.

The blade on the windscreen wiper of the grey Fiat made an unpleasant screech each time it swept from left to right, as if it was scratching the glass. He had got used to it and put it out of his mind, but the squeaks irritated the shaven-headed youngster sitting next to him.

'Can't you fix that crap?'

Calm down, Alfonso, he thought, without saying anything to him. Why are you always so nervous? Stay steady. Stop opening and closing the drum of your Magnum. Those steroids you're taking will drive you crazy.

'I know there are at least two pharmacies here,' said Guillermo, 'but I can't find them. Some bars in Brazil sell medicines too. Not everything, of course. But I've definitely seen them sell aspirin. Yet everything is shut here. In places like this people go to bed early.'

'Is the next town far from here?' Alfonso wanted to know.

'Not far,' said Guillermo. 'About thirty kilometres, perhaps forty. I can't remember. There are four towns close to each other. They're all small and very similar.'

'Let's go on to another one then. Stop driving round this ghost town.'

How peacefully he's sleeping, even with the fever, thought Emiliano, feeling the boy's hot forehead. He's hardly moving. The fever seems to have got worse. He's looking paler. He doesn't open his eyes. His hair is soaked with sweat, and so are his clothes. We don't have any others. He needs to take some kind of pill. It's cold in here. There's no fireplace in this house, no wood fire, nothing to warm things up. Why do the Brazilians build houses with no heating in cold places like this? What can they be thinking? Do they think summer lasts all year long? What am I supposed to do with this feverish kid? Whenever my son had a fever, his mother used to put him in a cold bath. And he often had fevers. Right up to the end. A sad kid. Sad mother. Sad the whole thing. I couldn't give a shit about sadness. Fuck sadness. Sadness can go and fuck itself. They can all go fuck themselves. All of them, every one of them. Go fuck themselves.

The Uruguayan went over to the bed in the corner of the room, picked up the blankets and sheets on it, brought them over and covered the boy. He wiped his forehead and hair.

Why don't we have any other clothes for him? Why didn't we think of buying them when we knew he might be with us for many days? Or weeks, until his father pays the ransom we're demanding? Why didn't Daniel tell them to buy some new clothes? An adult can wear the same clothes for I don't know how long, a long time, without changing. But a kid shits himself, pees his pants, gets himself dirty, like this one did. How long was Daniel planning for us to keep him? Why didn't we take him straight to Paraguay? Why didn't we keep him there, where we have more control over things, where we've already taken other prisoners and where we have good relations with the authorities we've bribed, until the time comes to hand him back?

What are Daniel and the Brazilian really planning to do with this kid?

Her first four attempts to speak to her father's employers got nowhere. The first time, there was no answer. In the next one, they slammed the phone down on her; in the third she wasted her time with a half-deaf old woman; the fourth was answered by a tearful young child who said she was all alone at home and was hungry.

Crouched under the telephone hood, feeling the cold more intensely because her clothes were soaked by the fine rain that kept on falling, Barbara was trying the number on the piece of cigarette paper the Major had given her. Each time she changed the last blurred digit. It could be a three, an eight, perhaps a six, or a seven, or a five. This last number was the only one left for her to try.

She would have called a lawyer if she had known one. She was sure her father was not involved with any drug traffickers. She was sure he could not have been. Because of how he was, and because no corrupt policeman would live so modestly.

She was sure of it. His employers would help her find a lawyer. She was sure they would help. They would testify to his good behaviour. She was sure of it. And she had no alternative.

She put another token in the public telephone. She heard it ring at the other end. She counted it ringing eight times. Then there was a click. A recorded message began to play, in English with an American accent: *We're sorry we can't take your call right now. Please record your message after the beep and we'll call you back as soon as possible.*

When she heard this foreign language Barbara was surprised and intimidated. She put the phone down without leaving any message.

She had one token left. She could not see a newspaper kiosk or bar open nearby where she could buy some more.

One token.

One last try.

God, if you exist, save my son. Show your face, God. Prove it isn't true that people like me are only here to work, have children, buy a refrigerator, work, cultivate a scrap of land, work and work until we die, live with the constant fear of poverty and hunger, and then one day die writhing in pain, a hole gnawing at our guts, the same hole that killed my mother and the one my boy emerged from, the poor, tiny, pale, defenceless boy I never wanted, oh God. Don't let him die, God. Or yes, let him, if that is better for him. If you didn't take

him when I wanted to get rid of him, when he was in my belly,
God, why are you forcing the child to go through what he is
going through now? Was it me who caused him to be born the
way he is, God? Or was it you, O Lord, was it you who wanted
to punish me, to remind me of the evil I did, when I tried all
those ways to get rid of him, God? Talk to me, God. Answer
my question: was it because of what I did that he was born like
this? Am I the one who's responsible? Or are you, Lord, trying
to show me that you exist and that you are going to punish me
for the rest of my days on earth, do you want me to learn that
I must suffer, God, suffer a lot, before I die and go to your
world, if that exists, God, God, talk to me. Talk to me. Say
something. Give me a sign. You who gave Moses a sign, who
set fire to the bush to prove that you exist, you who took the
knife out of Abraham's hands before he could plunge it into
Isaac's heart, you, O Lord, do not do this to my child. God.
Don't let him, God, don't let him suffer. If you intend to kill
my Isaac, Lord, don't let him suffer. Make it a quick death.
Don't let them suffocate the boy, or beat him, or drown him,
God, don't let them. You had a mother, you know how much
she loved you: that is how I love my own son. I know he is less
than the others, you were a son who made his mother proud,
the intelligent son who multiplied the bread and fishes: my
son can't even count, he has no idea what it means, God. But
he's a good child, a kind, good boy, who smiles at me and fixes
me with those chalky-blue eyes of his so that I think there
must be a reason that I had a child like him, God, there must
be a reason – I don't know what it is, but there must be one.

I don't care if I suffer, God. You can make me suffer, I don't care. I have never cared. You can set me to work from morning to night, you can have me marry a man who doesn't love me, you can give me pains in the stomach all day long, you can let me grow fat, and more wrinkled, and more ugly, I don't care at all, O Lord, all that is only the nonsense of the world of my employers.

But the boy! Don't hurt him, he is not to blame that his father doesn't love him, that everybody laughs at him, that his mind can never settle on anything, please do not hurt him, God. Hurt me. Let me feel all the pain those bandits are going to inflict on him. Don't let them cut off one of his ears or his toes, my God, if you exist, if you exist, Lord, save him, show that you are powerful, God, save him. Save him. For the love of the mother who gave you birth, save him.

The pharmacist was just pulling down the metal shutter when the small car pulled up opposite him. The indigenous-looking driver asked if he had something for a fever even before he got out of the vehicle. He spoke Portuguese with a Spanish accent. The front-seat passenger stayed in the car. He looked big, and was either completely bald or had a shaven head.

'Do you have a cold or some kind of inflammation?' the pharmacist asked, leaving the shutter half closed. 'If it's a throat problem or an inflamed tooth, an antibiotic would be better.'

'It's not for me. It's just a fever.'

'How bad is it?' insisted the pharmacist.

'I think it's quite bad.'

'A child or an adult?'

'An old man,' replied Guillermo after a moment's hesitation.

'Then it's better to give him something to bring his temperature down and combine it with this antibiotic. It works more quickly. When the fever starts to come down, keep on giving him the antibiotic, every three hours on the first day, every six on the next day, and every twelve hours for two more days.'

Guillermo paid for the two boxes of pills and the two envelopes of fever-reducing sachets. He was on his way out when he remembered the thermometer. He went back, asked for one, took it, paid. Before driving off, he asked from within the car where he could buy cigarettes. The pharmacist told him.

He found the open bar two blocks further on in a side street. There was no mistaking it: it was the only place with any lights on. Only one of the tables was occupied. The two customers, with a bottle of beer in front of them and half-filled glasses, were silent, staring at the television hanging on the wall on a metal support.

He went straight to the counter, and asked for two packs of the brand of cigarettes the Chilean had indicated. The barman did not seem to hear him. Guillermo saw that the blank-faced youth was also staring at the TV. He repeated his request. The boy seemed to wake up, and went to a small glass case, took out the cigarettes, handed them over, received payment and went back to watching the television.

Guillermo was walking out of the bar when he heard the presenter say the word: *Kidnap*. He turned round.

The image on the screen showed a dark, paunchy man standing next to a woman as blonde as the feverish boy at the farm. Between them was a boy as dark-skinned as the adult man. The camera zoomed in on the dark-haired boy. The announcer said that the son of the advertising executive Olavo Bettencourt had been abducted by drug traffickers in a lightning attack in a wealthy area of São Paulo. The kidnappers were working in tandem with the driver, Carlos Roberto da Costa, a former military policeman who was currently on the run. A photograph of the driver in military uniform appeared on screen. The images that followed were of soldiers and armed police officers entering a *favela*. 'The search for the kidnappers is continuing and will do so tomorrow morning,' said the announcer. 'We will not rest until we find the criminals and the boy Olavo Bettencourt Junior,' said a man in a dark suit. The photograph of the kidnapped boy appeared once more: he was dark-skinned, with a long face and black hair and eyes.

The recorded message came on again after the telephone had rung eight times. Barbara waited for the tone at the end of the words in English and said: 'My name is Barbara, and I'm the Major's daughter. He works as a driver for you, and I wanted to know how I can get in touch with him. The police have been to our home and told my mother he's under arrest, but they didn't say where they were holding him, or how we can talk to him and find out what's going on, and since my mother and I don't know any lawyers, and my stepfather has been arrested as well, and the Major, who is one of your drivers, I know my father cannot have anything to do with drug traffickers because my father, who works there, the Major, my father, who works there as a driver, he gave me this number to ring if I wanted to talk to him and I . . . I thought that . . . We've no idea who could help us over my father being arrested and . . . Please, if somebody there could help . . . please . . . I . . . I . . .'

'Are you the Major's daughter?' a woman's voice at the other end of the line said all of a sudden.

'Who's talking? Is that my father's employer?'

'I'm an employee,' said the woman. 'I'm the housekeeper, with my husband. I answered because I could hear you crying.'

'I'm not crying. I simply want to know about my father.'

'I don't know what they have done with him. They didn't say where they were taking his body.'

'Body? What body? What happened to my father?'

'I don't know who killed him. I don't know where they took him. I only answered because I know how much you must be suffering.'

'Where is my father? Where is he? Where?'

'Don't cry. That won't help. God doesn't hear.'

The phone went dead. Barbara stood with the receiver in her hand, listening to what sounded like a constant buzzing noise. Or a scream.

15

The study door was closed. Mara turned the knob once, twice, three times, until she realized it was locked. She knocked. Waited. Knocked again. Then started hammering.

Olavo opened it.

'I need to talk to you,' she said, pushing past him and into the room dominated by an enormous reproduction of the cover of a Captain America comic on a red wall, in front of which was a steel desk with a tinted glass top. Among the papers on it, she recognized the logo of one of the New York banks she occasionally visited with her husband. 'Were you calculating the money? For the ransom? Has Ernesto left? And the policeman as well?'

'He's an inspector, Mara. From the federal police. Yes, they've gone. It's all settled.'

'On television they're showing a photograph of us, together with Olavinho.'

'Hmm.'

'They're saying it was Olavinho who was kidnapped.'

'Hmm.'

'Why?'

'That's the strategy we decided on.'

'But what about the housekeepers' son? Why didn't they mention the little blond kid?'

'That's the strategy we adopted to gain time. Until the kidnappers are found.'

'Are you going to pay the kid's ransom? Are you going to take the money from that New York bank?' she asked, pointing to the statement on the desk. 'Is the number they left in the car the one for that account? Which account is the other number for? One of those in the Caribbean? How much are they demanding?'

'They want what's in the account, Mara.'

'How much?'

'All of it. Transferred from my Israeli bank account to theirs in the same bank. That was the meaning of their message.'

'All of it?'

'Don't worry. It's not your problem. The police will find them. There'll be a shoot-out. They'll all be killed in the exchange of fire.'

'And the kid?'

'What about the boy?'

'What's going to happen to the kid?'

'The same as every time a child is kidnapped. The same that happened to the son of a Japanese-Brazilian businessman here in São Paulo. The same as what they did to that daughter of the pharmaceutical company owner in Minas Gerais. And lots of other children. Here, in Italy, in India, in England. Children never come out of these things alive. Their parents know, the police know, everybody knows that, even if the ransom is paid, the kidnappers will kill the child. That's what happens in this kind of abduction.'

'But if you offered them a lot of money . . .'

'That boy isn't normal. He wouldn't have a future anyway.'

'The kid is . . . different. But if you—'

'What happens to him is unimportant. And it's not your problem.'

'We can save the kid, Olavo. He's worth less than Olavinho. A lot less. When the kidnappers learn he is the housekeepers' son, they'll accept whatever you offer.'

'*Whatever you offer*, Mara, whatever you offer. I haven't got anything to offer for that child.'

'I have.'

'Forget the boy, Mara.'

'I can sell the New York apartment and give them that money.'

'No, Mara.'

'The apartment is easy to sell.'

'No, Mara.'

'It's in a good location, a nice building, it has porters twenty-four hours a day, there's a laundry, and . . .'

'No, Mara.'

'It's on an upper floor, it has views, there are shops close by . . .'

'No.'

'It has a suite and a guest bathroom, it's a new building . . .'

'We can't sell the 72nd Street apartment.'

'Even if *you* don't want to save the boy's life, *I do*. The apartment must be worth around eight hundred thousand dollars. Wasn't that what you paid? I'm good with numbers, I have a good memory for them. Eight hundred and forty-five thousand dollars. I'll sell it and . . .'

'You can't sell the 72nd Street apartment.'

'Of course I can. Then you can negotiate with the kidnappers. They return the boy and . . .'

'I can't, Mara. We can't.'

'I can. I don't need your permission. The apartment belongs to me. You buy it in my name.'

'You *bought* it, Mara, you *bought* it.'

'I signed the papers. And I've got a copy of them.'

Olavo crossed behind her to the desk. He opened a drawer, took out some sheets of paper and held them out to Mara.

'Look at them again.'

She did not move.

'Look again, Mara. Read it, with the little English you know.'

'I'll take them to a lawyer.'

'He'll tell you it is a commodatum contract. You have the right to use the apartment whenever you want, as long as the owner agrees, for as long as it suits the owner, and providing that the owner does not have an immediate need for it when you ask to stay there.'

'In other words, as long as you agree.'

'It's not that simple.'

'What is it you wants?'

'It's amazing how you forget your grammar when you're

153

angry, like a real southern cowgirl, Mara. If you weren't white, blonde and blue-eyed, you could easily, so easily be a slut from a Rio de Janeiro slum.'

'Who did you buy the New York apartment for?'

'For no one, Mara. It's not a simple story of another lover. The 72nd Street apartment doesn't belong to me. Neither to me, nor to you.'

'I signed the contracts.'

'These. Of the commodatum contract. If you knew English, you would have seen that.'

'Who then . . . ?'

'It's owned by an account holder in a bank with head-quarters in Tel Aviv. A Brazilian government minister. Someone to whom I owe favours, publicity accounts, tips for tenders for publicity campaigns for firms that depend on government approval, all the complex world that little blonde head of yours will never understand.'

'I may not understand, Olavo. Not all the details. But journalists do. Any journalist I get in touch with will understand. I know the numbers of our bank account in New York by heart.'

'I can change those numbers with a phone call right now.'

'I know a lot about your deals with Ernesto and those friends of yours in Brasília.'

'Don't threaten me, Mara. You're pretty, you're the woman who excites me most, but you're an idiot, Mara. You're just dumb.'

'Call that minister, Olavo. Tell him you need that money now. Ask for nine hundred thousand dollars.'

'Mara Elizabeth Grunnert Bettencourt, my beloved wife and mother of my son, I'm the one who gives the orders here.'

'Tell that minister to arrange the money to free the kid from the kidnappers. Today. Now! This minute. Pick up the phone and call him, Olavo! Call him, call him, Olavo! Now. Now!'

Olavo put the contract back in the drawer and locked it. Then he sat down, cupped his head in his hands, and smiled.

'What kind of tone is that, Mara Elizabeth Grunnert Bettencourt?'

'I'm not going to let that boy die. Call the minister. Tell him you want the money immediately. Call him! Go on!'

'At this precise moment,' Olavo pushed back the sleeve of his Brooks Brothers shirt and checked the time on his Cartier watch, bought in a boutique on the Place Vendôme, 'the minister is travelling first class on a Varig Boeing 747, accompanied by the president of the republic and several close, trusted ministers. They are on their way to Manhattan, where tomorrow they will attend the opening session of the UN General Assembly, and in the evening, the minister will be fêted at a gala dinner, followed by a dance, as "Man of the Year" by the powerful association of North American business leaders who run industries in our country, as well as others who are making, or have already made, substantial investments in Brazil. It's impossible to talk to the minister at this moment. And, even if it were possible, the minister does not have the time, or the inclination, to worry about the fate a gang of bandits might want to inflict on a mentally retarded boy, the son of semi-literate housekeepers, kidnapped by mistake instead of his employer's son. Get out of here, Mara. You're disturbing me. I've got a hard-on, but I can't fuck you now. I have things to prepare before our trip.'

'What trip?'

'Didn't I tell you we're going to New York? We're leaving the day after tomorrow. Or rather . . .' he consulted his wristwatch again, '. . . tomorrow. On Wednesday night. We're going to join the president's entourage. Pack a case with the essentials. Cosmetics, underwear, things like that. Don't worry about what to wear at the parties and dinners. I'll buy you some new clothes.'

'But Olavo, the boy . . . The kidnappers are still . . .'

'The case will be solved within the next few hours. It's in the hands of the federal police and the government intelligence services.'

'I don't want to go.'

'You don't say "I Don't Want To" to me. You're going. I need your signature on some papers I have to deal with in Manhattan.'

'I don't want to.'

'You do. I want to, and therefore so do you. Now get out of here.'

Her initial reaction was to obey. But something kept her standing there, still close to the door of the red-walled study. She didn't recognize the feeling. It was new to her.

'No.'

'No what, Mara Elizabeth?'

'I'm not leaving here. I'm not going to New York. I'm not going to sign any documents. I'm not going to do what you want. I'm not going to do what you tell me to. I'm not going to do anything.'

'You're not?'

'No.'

'My dearly beloved Mara Elizabeth, this isn't a power struggle. Simply because you don't have any, and I have it all. That designer-label dress, those shoes, that well-groomed hair of yours, those manicured nails, your blemish-free skin, those teeth with their porcelain crowns, everything about you, everything that you are, is not yours. None of it belongs to you, Mara Elizabeth Grunnert Bettencourt. I pay for it all. I pay for you. To have you. To penetrate you whenever I want to. In your cunt, your arse, your mouth. Wherever and whenever I want. We're going to New York tomorrow. Now, get out of here.'

'No.'

'No?'

'No, Olavo, no. I'm not going to. I don't want to. I'm not going to New York. I'm not signing anything more.'

'No?'

'No. I already said no.'

'Then come here,' he said, standing up, undoing his flies and pulling out his penis. 'Come here and suck me off.'

Mara stood stock still.

'Come here.'

They were less than two metres from each other. Neither of them moved, each waiting for their adversary to take the first step.

'Suck me,' he ordered her.

'No,' Mara finally managed to say with conviction, for the first time since the first moment they had met and she began the game of pretending to try to escape from Olavo to arouse his desire for conquest and acquisition. Now the rule was broken. But he did not believe it.

'Suck me,' he repeated, easing his balls out of his trousers. 'Suck all of it. Right now.'

She felt like slapping him, but restrained herself. She folded her arms, pressed them to her sides. She took a deep breath.

'The newspapers and magazines,' she said in a trembling voice, 'will to want to know that the most powerful minister in the government has secret dealings with the most respected advertising man in Brazil.'

'And with some of the least respected as well. And not only abroad. Where do you think the money came from to pay for this house, the staff, the security guards, the drivers? How do you think the beach house you enjoy so much was paid for? And the apartment I gave your mother in Porto Alegre? You can tell all that to the journalists, Mara. Or would you prefer me to call you Natasha? Or Vanessa? Or Tamara? Or Isadora? Which of those names did you prefer when you were a call girl? I can see that you're surprised at what I know about your past, about what you did before hooking me with that tale of being engaged to an engineer who you were going to marry.'

'I never . . . I was never, I wasn't. You're only saying that because you're angry with me.'

'I'm not angry with you, Mara. Or would you prefer me to call you Ingrid? The lion is never angry with its prey. The lion loves its prey. He loves the gazelle that desperately flees him. I love you, Mara. I love you, Susana. Jackie. Francesca.'

'I never . . .'

'Don't be a hypocrite, Gisele. Letícia. Tatiana. Angela.'

'I was a model. I wasn't . . .'

'A call girl. No, Nathalie. You were an escort, Martina. A gentleman's escort, Caroline. You used to come from Porto Alegre to São Paulo or Rio de Janeiro. Occasionally you went to Brasília, Vera. Only a few times. To Goiania as well, Karine. And to Salvador. And if I'm not mistaken, to Recife, Rosana. You can tell all that to the journalists, Mirella. I can help, providing them with photos of your meetings.'

'You don't . . .'

'I do, Stephanie. I have lots of photographs. And a video, recorded in a motel in Rio.'

'You knew all the time.'

'Yes, Roberta, I knew. Yes, Renata, I knew. Yes, Flavia, I knew. Yes, Tania, Soraya, Nicole, Fernanda, Rafaela, Sandra, Marcela, Lia, Camila.'

'You knew.'

'Yes, Alessandra.'

'You knew from the start.'

'A little after the start. Yes, Carol, I knew. Yes, Paula, Diana, Andressa, Simone, Denise. Yes. I have the investigators' reports, the names of your clients, telephone numbers, photographs, everything. I can give copies to the journalists, if you wish.'

'You wouldn't do that.'

'Yes, Sandra, I would. Without hesitation. To defend my son, the future of my son and my wealth and his, I would not hesitate a moment, Giovanna. I would be the target of gossip for a while, then the interest would fade. With my money, my reputation and my network of contacts, everybody would soon be willing to forget I was once married to a whore.'

'I'm not a whore.'

'Yes, you are. And that's why I love you. Because you are a tramp, because I don't need to respect you, because of how common you are; all that and your pink cunt excites me. Always. Always, Mara. My gazelle. And you love me as well. For my money, for my proximity to power, for everything you always wanted and I gave you, for the pain I inflict on you. Those needs give you direction. And I'm the one who can satisfy them. It's me. I'm your compass, Mara Elizabeth Grunnert Bettencourt. Without me, you would career around like an out-of-control car.'

Accustomed to dissimulating and the masks behind which she hid even from herself, Mara lost all sense of where her indignation should take her. She was not accustomed to using truth as her weapon. She knew that she wanted to save the boy, and could still feel the discomfort, the shame and the pain of Olavo's finger digging inside her. But she could not get beyond that. She had no idea how to confront this man she had been living with for five years as a real person. She had always played a role, and sometimes almost believed in it. She had no idea who her real self might be.

'Go to sleep, my darling. It's past midnight. Don't worry about packing a bag for your journey. I'll tell Irene what to put in. Good night.'

16

Monday 20 August, 22.51

ALFONSO SNAPPED OPEN the Magnum .357 with his right hand, took the bullets out one by one and placed them between his legs. Then he pushed them back into their chambers, snapped the gun shut, opened it with his left hand, took out each bullet once more, repeated the same process. He went on doing this, first with one hand and then the other, judging his own agility, throughout all the drive back to the farm. He did not talk to Guillermo, who was not interested in speaking to him either. This was how they had always behaved since their first job together, four years earlier, when Daniel had hired them to get rid of a journalist who was making trouble for coca farmers in Bolivia. And they would behave in exactly the same way on their next mission, in Bogotá, when they were to abduct the heiress of a Colombian millionaire pepper exporter who was madly in love with a left-wing professor and was financing the activities of the terrorist group he belonged to.

They tolerated rather than liked each other, with an undercurrent of mutual disdain. The mental vacuum where

Alfonso floated made Guillermo as uncomfortable as the Yamana Indian's quick-wittedness disturbed the great-great-grandson of Irish settlers who had usurped the land of Guillermo's ancestors in the south of Argentina, where they had been taken by Anglican missionaries. They worked together quickly and efficiently. They made a well-balanced team. They did not make mistakes. They left no traces. And they shared the habit of silence: neither of them felt the need to talk.

And yet in the early hours of that morning there was nothing routine about Guillermo's muteness.

He opened the gate himself, drove the car through, got out again and closed it. Alfonso stopped juggling with his gun, held it in his more accurate left hand, and cradled it on his thigh.

Before they made their way up the track to the house, Guillermo switched the light on inside the car. The Peruvian on guard on the veranda relaxed, lowered the rifle he had been aiming at them and sat down again on the wooden bench.

Guillermo parked alongside the Kadett, waited for Alfonso to get out, picked up the cigarettes and medicines from the back seat, closed the windows and locked the car. He set off up to the farmhouse.

He was trying to connect what seemed to him like random points.

By the time he got there, Alfonso was already sprawled on the only sofa, eyes closed and hands inside his woollen jacket. It was as cold indoors as it was out in the open. The door to the room Daniel reserved for himself was closed. He was probably asleep. He had no reason to worry. Everything was going to plan. The Brazilian would arrive in the morning, in the same vehicle that Alfonso and Guillermo were to use to return to São Paulo. There, according to their plans, they would send the cassette with the voice and sobs of the adman's son. Then they were to take separate flights to Asunción and Buenos Aires, where they were to await instructions to set Operation Bogotá in motion.

Guillermo went to the room where the boy was being kept, and opened the door. All he could see in the bed was a small heap of blankets, with no sign of a head or feet. He took two steps forward, and was about to raise the blanket when he felt the cold barrel of the Uruguayan's pistol against his temple. He came to a halt.

'I want to see the child's face,' he said, without turning round.

'Why?' asked Emiliano, still pressing the 9mm Walther to the ruddy-cheeked Indian's face.

'I've brought the medicines you asked for. And the thermometer.'

'Leave them there.'

'Why have you got the gun to my head?'

'You were walking like an Indian towards an enemy.'

'Are you nervous, Uruguayan?'

'Give me the medicines.'

Taking the bag, he tucked the Walther into his waistband.

'What's this?'

'It's an antibiotic. The pharmacist said the boy could have an inflammation.'

'Did you mention the boy to the pharmacist?' Emiliano asked angrily.

'Of course not. Do you think I'm as stupid as Alfonso?' he said, then added: 'I said an old guy had a fever.'

'There was no point buying it. You can't give a child adult antibiotics. Get out, Bolivian.'

'You know I'm not Bolivian. I'm Argentine.'

'You look like a Bolivian. The Organization in Santiago calls you the Bolivian.'

'I'm Argentine.'

'All right, so tell me who wrote these verses: "*Now the sea is a long separation between ashes and the homeland. Now all of life, however humble, can tread its nothing and its night. Now God will have forgotten him, and it is less an insult than compassion to postpone his infinite dissolution with charitable coins of hatred.*"'

'I don't know any poetry. I didn't study much. What does "infinite solution" mean?'

'What about these lines, Bolivian,' he challenged him: '"*Nobody fails, no one stands out, criminals are just like us, some live a lie, others in their ambition rob, it's all the same to be a priest, upholsterer, the King of Clubs, a shameless rogue, or down-at-heel.*"'

'I don't know that either.'

'How can you be Argentine if you don't recognize either Borges or tangos?'

'It's only white Argentines who like tango. And was Borges the blind guy?'

'You talk like a Bolivian. Your accent is different.'

'So is yours. So do you.'

'I'm Uruguayan, damn it.'

'Uruguayans talk like Argentines.'

'Like shit we talk like them. We have Catalan and Andalusian blood in our veins. The Argentines don't know how to speak Spanish. They sound like Italians.'

'I don't talk like an Italian. And I'm as Argentine as Alfonso. More so, in fact. My people were there long before his gringo relatives arrived. I want to see the boy's face.'

'Why?'

'How many sons does the advertising man have, Uruguayan?'

'I don't know. Three, or two. Ask Daniel. He will know.'

'Three or two?'

'Three or two, what difference does that make, damn it?'

'Did you see the other sons?'

'I only saw this one.'

'When?'

'What's that to you, damn it? I saw this son, with his mother, at the school entrance. You saw them as well.'

'Yes, I saw them. She was tall and blonde. She carried him. Yes, I saw them. But just now, on the television, the boy they showed was . . .'

'Fuck the television. Bring a glass of water. I'm going to dissolve these powders and give them to him.' His fever is getting worse by the hour, he said to himself after Guillermo had left the room, untangling the blankets and slipping the thermometer into the boy's mouth.

His eyes were still closed. He was shivering. Sweating.

Tuesday 21 August, 01.03

In the metro carriage the thin young woman with wet clothes and hair was clinging to her rucksack as if it was a lifebuoy in a shipwreck. She was trying to keep her spirits up, but felt she was being swept along by currents that were beyond her comprehension. She was struggling to breathe, like someone swallowing water when they are trying to take in more air.

He's dead. That's what the woman said. She said she didn't know where his body had been taken. His body. My father's body. He wasn't arrested. He's not arrested. He is dead. My father is dead. They killed my father. The police killed my father. Was it the police who killed my father? Why did the police kill my father? Did the police assassinate my father? Who assassinated my father? Why did they assassinate my father? Why did they say he is a drug trafficker? Was he a drug trafficker? That he was the accomplice of traffickers? Who killed him? Why was he killed? Why did they kill him? When did they kill him? How did they kill him? Where? Did he suffer? Did my father have a painful death? He didn't deserve to meet a painful death. My father didn't deserve to die. Not like that. Like what? Who decides that a person is to die because somebody else says he's a drug trafficker? Where did they take my father's body? Where is my father's body? Who can help me find my father's body? Nobody can help me find it. Why did they make my father's body disappear? How could they . . . Who took the body? Why did the police go to my house and search it, breaking things and scaring my mother? Why did they smash everything in my house? How can they get into a house, search everywhere and break everything? How can they do that? Why can they?

They came in. They searched. They broke things. And took away my stepfather. Why did they take him? Who says that he is a drug trafficker, as they are saying my father is? Or was. How could they kill my father? How could they kill someone without anybody knowing? How can they do that to him? How can they do that to people? Who can do it? Who gives the order? Who is in command? Who says that such and such a person can be killed? Or somebody else? How can they get into people's houses, terrify us, make us think we're guilty of a crime we're unaware of? Why am I scared if I'm so angry at them? Why do I feel they have no right to do this, and yet am scared they might do even worse things to us? How can they do that to people? Who allows it? Why do they have the power to do that to people? Who are they? Who are they? Who?

Barbara did not notice that tears were streaming down her face.

When the metro stopped at Barra Funda station, she jumped out. She was dizzy ... She leaned against a pillar. Then she began to sob. She let her body slide down, sat still on the ground, openly weeping, oblivious to the few passengers who were about at this time of night. She finally calmed down.

She stood up. With the anxiety of someone surfacing. She would survive.

She would survive.

And would made a decision: she no longer wanted to live in

this country where she had no rights. She would emigrate to the United States. As Luís Cláudio was planning to do, as his brother had done, as so many other Brazilians were doing. She would emigrate. Yes, she would emigrate. Goodbye, Brazil. Goodbye, dirty tricks. Goodbye, corruption. Goodbye, poverty, goodbye prices that go up every day, goodbye fear of the police, goodbye Barra Funda, goodbye São Paulo, goodbye mother, goodbye everything, goodbye everyone, goodbye for ever, goodbye, goodbye, goodbye. A cleaner here, a cleaner there, what's the difference? And she would be earning in dollars. The person who faked the visa on her passport could also fake her date of birth. She would increase her age to eighteen. Nineteen. Tomorrow, in the English course, she would talk to Luís Cláudio. Perhaps she could go with him. Yes, she would go with him. Tomorrow morning she would arrange everything with Luís Cláudio. They would leave together for Canada and from there go to the city close to Boston where so many Brazilians lived. Tomorrow. Or rather, today: it was past one in the morning.

The wardrobe was still open in front of her, with the rows of dresses, blouses, coats, jackets, skirts, different-coloured sashes, organized by Olavo in careful combinations so that in the circles where he showed her off nothing would ever clash in the elegant young lady he had created. At the back and on the sliding doors, two-metre-high mirrors allowed her to see herself from all angles.

What she saw was: a tall woman, made to look even taller by her high-heeled shoes, with long legs, narrow hips, breasts slightly larger than might have been expected in someone with such a slender frame. She was wearing a long-sleeved beige shirt with the collar raised, done up at the front with buttons covered in the same material, and fastened at the waist with a grey sash, one of those thick golden chains with several strands round her elongated neck, emphasized by her hair done up in a bun, and pearl studs in the lobes of her small ears. She looked like that Hollywood actress who became princess of Monaco. Just like Olavo had wanted and moulded her to be.

She slowly unrolled the Versace chain, and let it drop. It made no sound as it fell to the thick vanilla-coloured carpet. She unscrewed the Cartier ear-studs. She dropped them to the floor as well. They made no noise either. The silence that reigned in this room with white walls, white furniture, white duvet, white blinds and curtains, only increased her impression that she was floating in a huge, empty womb. She loosened her bun. Her hair fell to her shoulders. She took off her Gucci shoes. Undid the Dior sash. Threw it over the row of charcoal grey and white Chanel-style tailored suits. She undid the buttons of her Saint-Laurent blouse one by one, let it slide down to her bare feet. She had nothing on underneath.

What she saw now in the mirrors: a lanky, thin and frail young girl, her ribs sticking out under her skin, her hair cut very short because of the nits at her school, stomach rumbling with hunger but disgusted at the thought of food, her eyes sunk so deep in her face that their chalky-blue colour was barely visible, a first light-blond down starting to cover the area at the top of her thin legs.

Feeling ashamed, the woman in front of the mirror covered her sex and shielded her breasts behind one arm.

He drove slowly up the hill, flashing the headlights of the black saloon especially adapted for invalids. He wanted to reassure the man on guard. In the dark and rain, he could barely make out the silhouette traced by the veranda light, but he knew that whoever it was would have an AK-47 trained on him, with their finger on the trigger. At less than three hundred metres, the weapon brought to Brazil via Paraguay could pierce the Passat GTS Pointer he had bought with what was left of his long-service pension, and riddle his body with six hundred bullets in less than a minute. A gloomy thought. A beautiful weapon. One of the few good things the Communists made without copying the democratic world.

By the time he parked alongside the two smaller cars, Daniel was already at the farmhouse door, peering out. Then a taller, shaven-headed figure came and stood behind him. The Indian moved in front of them, jumped down the step, and took up position next to the Peruvian. They all had their weapons at the ready.

It occurred to him that, lined up as they were, he could mow them all down with one burst of his semi-automatic.

The idea would have amused him if he had not been so furious. The only one he could not see was the Uruguayan. He must be sleeping, the way old folk do all the time.

He opened the car door, pulled the folded-up wheelchair from the back seat and set it effortlessly on the gravel. Unfolding the chair, he moved from the driver's seat into it with surprising agility for a 45-year-old man who weighed more than eighty kilos. He slammed the door.

What he did find difficult was to make the wheels move on the mixture of mud and gravel.

'Bring him here,' ordered Daniel.

'I don't need any help, damn it,' he protested to no avail, when Alfonso and the Peruvian lifted his chair and carried him into the house.

'It's cold in here, and dark.'

'There's no fireplace in the house,' Daniel said, turning up the lamp on the table. 'And no electricity for radiators. You know this isn't a luxury ranch. We were expecting you tomorrow. What's happened? Why did you come now?'

'Because you're an arsehole.'

Daniel stiffened: 'What was that you said?'

'I said you're an arsehole. You're all arseholes.'

Alfonso took a step forward.

'Put that weapon down, Argie. Don't try playing the macho with me. I may be in this wheelchair but I'll snap you in two before you can so much as blink. I've dealt with people twice as big and tough as you. Here, in Uruguay, in Chile and in your country as well. Ask Daniel. I can make you cry from more pain than you ever thought it was possible to feel. Pain so great you'll ask me to kill you so you don't suffer any more.'

Daniel lifted his chin, and Alfonso lowered his Magnum .357 and stepped back.

'You could be the most stupid of all, Argie. But one of us is even more of a jerk.'

He paused theatrically, melodramatically, just like in the good old days of the long, painstaking interrogations of journalists, trade unionists and workers that he had directed in Rua Tutoia. That was before they were suspended and then closed down after President Geisel had sacked General D'Avila Mello because of the scandal created by the subversive press in the wake of the death of that Jew Herzog in the military torture centre.

'The biggest jerk here is me.'

He paused again. The four men waited for him to explain. Antonio preferred to take his time. He did not allow his anger to show: he was using it to reassert his authority, which he should never have allowed to slip from him. He had information that would decide the futures of all the men there.

'As well as the federal police, they've now brought in the São Paulo military and civilian police forces to search for the child. That's good. We have reliable informers within the civilian police. Thanks to them I've learned that the kidnappers of the adman's son are five drug traffickers from the *favelas* on the outskirts of São Paulo. The police have already raided one of their hideouts. They killed two kidnappers who were resisting arrest. They are pursuing another two. They will be found by the end of the morning. Doubtless they will confront the police, they'll exchange fire, and will prefer death to prison. That was what my informers told me. They also told me that the head of the gang, the bandit who planned the whole thing, is a former military policeman who worked as a driver for the adman's wife. He knew the family's routine, and passed all this information to the traffickers. He's also on the run. And he is as dangerous or more so than his accomplices.'

Daniel realized that Antonio was inverting roles. Like a good, experienced strategist, he was respecting the balance of forces until he could define his own position more clearly.

'Do you mean the driver Alfonso neutralized?'

'Yes, Daniel. The man whose spinal chord Alfonso severed.'

'I don't get it,' said Leonel the Peruvian, who rarely spoke.

'Nor do I. I fired into his chest.'

'And one in each shoulder,' Guillermo recalled.

'Tell us what's going on,' said Emiliano, appearing in the bedroom doorway. 'What's all this about traffickers? Why did you come here?' he added, closing the door behind him.

'No one is searching for us, Uruguayan. And no one will. The police don't hunt stupid jerks like us.'

'What the fuck are you talking about?' shouted Emiliano. 'The jerk is your fucking whore of a mother, you Brazilian bastard.'

'A jerk is someone who kidnaps the wrong child,' shouted Antonio. 'A jerk is someone who doesn't realize that the adman was expecting some kind of operation like ours and changed his routine to take his son to school in his armour-plated car. A jerk is someone who doesn't investigate properly, allows himself to be fooled, and risks his life attacking the Mercedes that the housekeepers' son is travelling in. A jerk is the one who believed there would be two million, three hundred and seventy thousand dollars transferred from those government bastards' secret account into ours. The jerk is me. I'm the greatest jerk on earth. Worse than any of you, you useless cockroaches.'

None of them moved. None of them said a word. They all suddenly realized that their plans for a future with three hundred thousand dollars in their pockets, after discounting the five hundred thousand seven hundred and seventy-five dollars for the Organization in Santiago, had been blown to smithereens.

'Pack up everything. Each of you goes back to his base.

'You, the Peruvian, return to Lima via Mato Grosso and Bolivia. Take trains and buses. You, the Uruguayan, drive Alfonso to Porto Alegre in the Fiat. There he can catch a flight to Buenos Aires. You carry on to the border between Uruguaiana and Paso del León, burn the car, and from there catch a bus. You, the Bolivian, take the Kadett to Foz do Iguaçu, leave the car in Brazil, cross the Bridge of Friendship on foot. In Ciudad del Este in Paraguay, ask for a room at the Hotel Valenciano. The manager will give you the keys to a vehicle. Drive it to Asunción and wait. You, Daniel, come with me back to São Paulo.'

'Why?'

'I talked to the Organization in Santiago. That's what they want, and that's what you'll do.'

Daniel lowered his eyes, then looked up again. He gave each

of the others in the room a long, hard look, and they all returned his gaze. The complete silence was the admission of their failure.

'I'll get my things,' he said, turning his back on them and going into the bedroom.

'And the boy, are we going to leave him here?' asked Guillermo.

'There's a hydro-electric dam near here. Throw his body in, tied to something heavy. You do it, Alfonso. Put the boy out of his misery. But don't throw him in alive, that would be cruel.'

17

DAY HAD NOT yet dawned when a grey Fiat Uno built in 1989 and running on alcohol, with licence plates from Minas Gerais, reached the vast lake formed by the Paineiras dam and came to a halt in the picnic area.

The rain had eased off.

A boy lay quietly on the back seat wrapped in blankets. On the right in the front a thin, prematurely aged man stared at the faint lines of colour that were beginning to pierce the grey clouds in the sky, like a child's scribbles on scrap paper. The scrawls were reflected on the calm surface of the lake below them, where flocks of cormorants bobbed tranquilly.

The shaven-headed youngster next to him switched off the engine, took the long-barrelled revolver from his waistband and flicked off the safety catch.

Day had not yet dawned when the young woman with bedraggled hair got on to the metro at Barra Funda station together with hundreds of other passengers, indistinguishable among all the women and men weary from yet another night with too little sleep. She was heading for the centre of São Paulo, wearing a rucksack that was far too heavy for her frail body.

In it were books and notes for her course in secretarial English, an English–Portuguese dictionary she often consulted, a soap container, toothpaste and toothbrush, a white T-shirt to change into before she began her cleaning work, passport-sized photographs and identity documents she was going to give to Luís Cláudio when she asked him to help with a one-way trip to the United States.

She did not see, because she was never interested in them, the front pages of the newspapers dangling from the kiosk in the station. Two of them carried a photograph of her father, taken in the days when he was a military policeman. COP RAN DRUGS GANG read the headline in one. In another, the same photo but smaller sized appeared above the other one of four dead men, weapons scattered beside their bodies. KID-NAPPERS TAKE ON COPS AND DIE, read the headline.

Day had not yet dawned when the housekeeper in the Bettencourt family residence went into the kitchen and headed straight for one of the white Formica cupboards where she kept the Italian polished aluminium kettle with its copper spout. She didn't need to switch the light on, she could see well enough thanks to the glow coming through the window that gave on to the guard-post. She knew every centimetre of that room, which was twice the size of the entire house where she had spent her childhood in the interior of Santa Catarina state. She was going to boil water because she needed to be doing something. She had spent a sleepless night walking along the corridor linking the main house and the servants' quarters and her own room, and then out into the night towards the garage, and back to her room, treading softly so as not to disturb her husband Stephan's sleep or to wake anybody else. Until finally she could not bear walking up and down any more, and so washed her face, brushed her teeth and decided to start her day's work.

She heard a noise behind her, and immediately snapped on the light.

'Dona Mara,' she exclaimed in surprise when she saw her employer sitting at the kitchen table, head in hands.

The blonde woman, with her hair in a ponytail, raised her head. Her eyes were red and swollen.

'Dona Mara,' the housekeeper repeated, without knowing how to go on or what to say.

Day had not yet dawned when the two cars left the side road and turned on to the six-lane highway. There they headed in different directions. The maroon Chevrolet Kadett hatchback went south, towards Paraná state. The black Passat Pointer GTS took the Bandeirantes motorway to the west, towards São Paulo.

'We screwed up,' said the man with the oval face, his curly hair now smoothed down neatly to match the charcoal-grey suit, white shirt and navy-blue tie he was wearing. In the briefcase on his lap he was carrying a European Community passport that he was going to use to travel to Lisbon that night, as the Spanish citizen Rodolfo López Rubio, engineer by profession: the same one with which he had entered Brazil the last two times. From the Portuguese capital he intended to drive to Seville, on a mission he would learn the details of when he got there.

'But I learned we have a good market here in Brazil,' he went on, after waiting in vain for a response from Antonio. 'Very good. Not for huge operations like the one with the adman. That was too big. He was too close to powerful people in Brasília. But fine for other, smaller abductions. The owners of medium-sized companies, for example. There are so many of them here. The senior figures in charge of chains of stores. Brothers and sisters and other close relatives of country music stars or soccer players. Bus company bosses. There are so many of them, Antonio. So many. And families are so close here in Brazil.'

Irene turned her back, pretending she was looking for the kettle. She felt embarrassed at this display of weakness from Mara, and wanted to give her time to recover, so that she herself could think of the best way to act in a situation she found deeply disturbing.

Happiness is easy for this woman. She has money, she has this beautiful house, a good husband, she has an intelligent son, she has her health, she has everything nice and whatever she wants, and yet . . . and yet . . .

'Would ma'am like some coffee?' she asked, as she might have asked Do You Need Help if she had been talking to some-one of the same social class as her. She could sit next to the young blonde woman as if she was a neighbour, a cousin, a sister, and ask: Why Are You Crying? or: Can I Help in Any Way? She would say to her: I Tried to Cry the Whole Night Long But Could Not Find That Relief. Or: I Have a Hole in My Chest That Hurts So Much I Think I'm Going to Die. But in the end, all she said was:

'I'll put some water on to boil.'

Mara nodded. Irene poured two cupfuls of filtered water into the kettle, put it on the stove with eight burners, and lit the most powerful one. She took the coffee from the refrigerator where it was stored to keep it fresh, measured three spoonfuls into the paper filter, then placed that on a white china pot. 'I'm making it good and strong,' she said, avoiding looking directly at Mara.

The kettle soon started whistling through its copper spout. Irene poured the boiling water on the coffee.

'Would ma'am like it with milk?'

'I just want a small black one, Irene. And a cigarette.'

'I don't smoke, Dona Mara,' she apologized, holding out the sugar bowl. 'Sweetener or sugar?'

≈

181

Alfonso waved his revolver at the child on the back seat.

'No,' said Emiliano. 'Not me. You take care of that. You were the one Daniel said should do it.'

'Help me then.'

'What do you want me to do?'

'Go and find a big stone, or a bit of iron, something we can tie to his body so it sinks. That's what Daniel told us,' he reminded him, climbing out of the car and opening the rear door.

He still had the gun in his hand.

He grabbed the pile of blankets covering the boy.

'Wait, Alfonso. Let me lift him out.'

Alfonso agreed.

Emiliano got out of the Fiat, treading in the mud all round the parked car, and stood beside Alfonso.

'Stand back. I'll pick him up.'

The boy's feet, in a pair of Alfonso's thick woollen socks, were pointing towards the two men. Emiliano took hold of one end of the blanket and pulled the boy gently to him. Then, putting his hands beneath the boy's body, he lifted him on to his shoulder.

'Over there,' Alfonso signalled, pointing to a log used for mooring boats. 'Put him over there.'

Emiliano carried the boy closer to the water. His head, with the eyes still tight shut, lolled to one side when he left him propped against the length of wood on the muddy ground. He made no sound.

Emiliano walked away. He reached the edge of the lake. The first rays of the sun were forcing their way through the grey clouds, shining on the waters of the lake and picking out the details of the shore opposite to where they had parked.

Alfonso went up to the little boy.

He aimed his Magnum .357.

He hesitated.

'Head or body?' he wondered out loud. 'Where should I shoot him, *viejito*?'

There was no response.

'Better aim for the head,' Alfonso concluded, raising his gun again. 'It will be smashed to bits, and that'll make him more difficult to identify.'

A shot tore through the silence of the lake. Ducks flew up in panic.

Daniel had been thinking since early morning, and now presented his proposal to Antonio: 'We're going to continue to operate in the way the Organization in Santiago brought us together for.'

'What are you trying to say, Daniel?'

'We failed this time because it was too big for us, and we trod on the toes of people more powerful than we are. But here in Brazil there's a vast number of opportunities for us. We're in a huge free market. We can make bigger profits with smaller investments.'

'How's that?'

'If we operate more often but in less spectacular ways. There are excellent people in Chile: the ones who have been out of work ever since the fall of Pinochet. People who are good at kidnapping and keeping their victims captive for as long as necessary.'

'The Organization in Santiago is already employing them.'

'Not all of them. Not all the time. Think how many owners of steelworks there are just in São Paulo. Think how many big cattle ranchers there are in Mato Grosso do Sul. Think how many building contractors are working in Paraná. Think how many owners of stockbrokers, tourist agencies, jewellery stores, mining outfits there are . . . it's a limitless market.'

'What would we do with them?'

'Not with them, with their bank accounts. We wouldn't ask for much. Just enough to start filling our own accounts without emptying theirs. We wouldn't ask for absurd amounts. Their families would agree to pay the ransoms.'

Antonio liked the idea. Plans and images came flooding back into his mind. Miami. Mustang. Camaro. Coconut Grove.

'When I get back from this mission in Spain we can sort out the details. You'll be rich, Antonio. You and I will be. Afterwards, you could even live in the quiet, protected neighbourhood I live in outside Santiago.'

'Santiago has too many hills. It's not good for a wheelchair. I don't like Santiago. I don't want to live in Santiago. I want to live in Miami.'

'Miami,' Daniel wondered. 'How will you understand people in the States?' he said with a laugh. 'You can hardly speak any English.'

Antonio smiled as well. Along the side of the road the first unfinished shacks and wooden huts began to appear, the sign that they were approaching the city.

'That won't be a problem. Nobody in Miami speaks English.'

～

Seeing how lost Mara looked, Irene asked again: 'Sweetener or sugar?'

'Irene, I'm going to the United States tonight, and I need you to . . .'

'Doctor Olavo told me to prepare your case yesterday.'

'Yesterday? You knew yesterday that I . . . You knew before me that I was going to . . .'

'Is there anything special you would like me to add?'

'I need you to call this number.' Mara put a scrap of paper in Irene's hand. 'After Olavo and I have left. Without him knowing about it. Without anyone knowing about it. Call from a public phone booth.'

Irene saw a number and a man's name. She dropped the piece of paper on the table.

'No, Dona Mara. I'm sorry. I'm sorry, but I'm not going to make the call.' She refused, thinking it must be a lover. 'I can't do that to Doctor Olavo.'

'It's the editor of this magazine's number,' said Mara, realizing Irene's mistake. She pointed to the weekly magazine on the table that she had read and re-read many times that morning. 'He's campaigning against government corruption. You can take the piece of paper, Irene.'

'No, Dona Mara. I'm sorry. I won't make the call. I can't.'

185

'Please, Irene. Call and say who I am, and that I'll be in New York, at the banquet for the minister they are investigating.'

'No, Dona Mara. I can't do that. I don't know if I can.'

'Call and tell them I have information. That my husband is the one who makes purchases for the minister. That he has an apartment in New York, paid for with funds from the presidential campaign. Tell them the minister has a secret account, that I know about everything and want to talk to them. Tell them to send a reporter to look for me at the banquet.'

'I don't know if I can, Dona Mara.'

'Tell the reporter to come and find me tomorrow. That I will tell him everything.'

'Dona Mara . . . I'm frightened.'

'Me too, Irene. Me too.'

One shot was enough.

The arc traced by the nine-millimetre bullet, made in the US state of South Dakota between the last week of May and the first week of June 1989, pierced the glabella at a speed of three hundred metres per second and, smashing the frontal bone, sped through the cranium, destroying a hundred billion neurons as it passed through the cortex, the corpus callosum, blood vessels, thalamus, cerebellar vermis, pituitary gland, hypothalamus, hippocampus, amygdalas, temporal lobe, the entire mass of the cerebral hemispheres, the cerebellum and the brain stem, all the things that control reason and motor functions, the contraction of muscles, speech, hearing, sight, posture, balance, breathing, interests, fears, doubts, likes and dislikes, the wish to have a beer at the end of a long, hot summer's day, the choice of a football team or a favourite cartoon, the first phrase learned by heart and the first music sung, the fervent wish that the wolf wouldn't eat the three little piggies or Little Red Riding Hood, the ability to understand that two and two make four, the trip to neverland with fairy dust, the moment of ecstasy inside a woman's body, the favourite coloured pencils, the smell of baking bread spreading through a house, the pleasure of playing at hide-and-seek, being alert to danger, slipping off to sleep, the footballer's sway of the hips on the ball, the taste of honey as it dissolves on the tongue, the relief of emptying intestines and kidneys, amazement at the first sight of the sea, the burp over a soft drink and the shiver from a cold wind, the scratch of a speck of dust in the eye and the easing of hunger at the mother's breast, deceptions, surprises, laughter, tears, and all the memories, dreams, desires and hopes he would never have again.

The bullet exited through the parietal bone, leaving a round hole and converting two hundred thousand years of evolution into a shapeless mush.

Alfonso toppled over backwards, like a puppet with its strings cut. He lay still for ever, his back and shoulders covered in the mud from the previous night's rain, his right arm flung out beside his body, the left pointing towards Emiliano. His hand relaxed, and the silver Magnum .357 slid loose. A dark pool began to spread beneath his head, soaking his wool jacket and mixing with the mud. Almost no blood oozed out of the hole between his eyes that was little bigger than a fifty-cent coin.

On an impulse, Barbara got off the Red Line metro a stop before her destination. She wanted to take a last look at the square where she used to stroll with her parents on Sundays. As a little girl who had never left the concrete confines of the city, its lake and clumps of trees had made it seem to her like a vast country ranch.

She went up two floors, and out into the open air.

It was growing light. The rain had ceased.

She jumped over a puddle.

She took a deep breath, sensing the familiar, comforting smell enter her nostrils, a mixture of the sharp, cold morning air on that 21 August and the acrid fumes emitted by the thousands of buses and cars permanently circulating around this metropolis of ten million inhabitants, added to on this Tuesday morning by the smell of damp grass and earth in the badly tended flowerbeds in Praca da República.

This was her farewell.

A cold wind was blowing empty plastic bags, newspapers, leaves, crushed cigarette packets, the rubbish dropped on the pavements early that morning. A beer can rolled to her feet.

She pulled up her jacket collar to protect her neck, thrust her hands in the pockets of her jeans, and then strode across the square, heading for her English for Secretarial Work course in Rua Maria Paula, thirteen blocks away. Her mind was buzzing, registering every tree, bench, flowerbed, every rectangle of sky above her head, every kerb, traffic light, awning, every closed store, bus stop, every window, wall, graffiti, every torn poster, every rubbish bin, overwhelmed by the same feeling of freedom and apprehension she always felt.

She had become an adult.

Emiliano put away his weapon, bent down to pick up the boy, and carried him back to the car. Laying him on the back seat, he pulled back the dirty blanket, felt his forehead.

The fever had passed.

He dragged the blanket over to Alfonso's body and covered him. The hand with the Magnum was poking out.

'It's no use to you any more,' he said, picking it up.

Emiliano went back to the car, laid the weapons on the passenger seat, took off his coat, and was about to wrap it round the boy when he opened his eyes.

He did not seem frightened. He looked curiously at Emiliano for a few seconds. Then he tilted his head to one side and smiled.

Emiliano put the coat over his small frame. The boy smiled once more, grateful to the man who had helped ward off the cold.

'I'm going to leave you in a safe place, kid. Don't worry,' he said, getting into the car and driving off.

The boy closed his eyes again and fell fast asleep.

Edney Silvestre is a Brazilian writer and journalist whose work as a TV reporter has taken him to Iraq and to the 9/11 attacks in New York. He currently presents a popular TV book programme and lives in Rio de Janeiro. *Happiness is Easy* is his second novel. His bestselling first novel, *If I Close My Eyes Now*, also translated by Nick Caistor, is also available in paperback.

If I Close My Eyes Now

Edney Silvestre

A horrifying discovery by two young boys while playing in some mango groves marks the end of their childhood. As they open their eyes to the adult world, they see a place where storybook heroes don't exist, but villains and lies do . . .

'Sadistic sexual politics, investigated by an unlikely trio of
sleuths (two schoolboys and an elderly man); misogynistic
murder; syncretic Christianity; municipal shenanigans, all
fester beneath the raging Rio sun'
THE TABLET

'Silvestre's real subject is Brazil, "a country capable of
advancing fifty years in only five of full democracy", as it
lurches out of the developing world'
GUARDIAN